ANNA'S RETURN

Anna Silverton and Janek Dabrowski escape war-torn Europe together, forging a friendship that carries them through difficult times. Even when they are apart, Anna dreams of Janek coming for her so they can be a family. Then, when she is accused of harming her half-brother, Teddy, she runs away, finding Janek again. Their childhood friendship soon turns to a tentative love, but the vicious lies told about Anna force them to part once again. Can the couple ever have a future together?

*Books by Sally Quilford
in the Linford Romance Library:*

THE SECRET OF HELENA'S BAY
BELLA'S VINEYARD
A COLLECTOR OF HEARTS
MY TRUE COMPANION
AN IMITATION OF LOVE
SUNLIT SECRETS
MISTLETOE MYSTERY
OUR DAY WILL COME
BONFIRE MEMORIES
MIDNIGHT TRAIN
TAKE MY BREATH AWAY
THE GHOST OF CHRISTMAS PAST
TRUE LOVE WAYS

SALLY QUILFORD

ANNA'S RETURN

Complete and Unabridged

LINFORD
Leicester

First published in Great Britain in 2013

First Linford Edition
published 2014

A catalogue record for this book is available
from the British Library.

ISBN 978–1–4448–2191–8

Published by
F. A. Thorpe (Publishing)
Anstey, Leicestershire

Set by Words & Graphics Ltd.
Anstey, Leicestershire
Printed and bound in Great Britain by
T. J. International Ltd., Padstow, Cornwall

This book is printed on acid-free paper

1

Janek estimated that the little girl could not have been more than eight years old, yet she seemed to be alone. She sat opposite him on the train, staring out of the window with sad blue eyes. Occasionally her head turned slightly and she stole a glance at him. She clutched a small satchel in her hand, and under her seat was a suitcase that was almost as big as her.

He supposed he must look very frightening to her. Weeks without proper food had left him very thin. He did not want to scare her, but the reason he sat in that carriage was because he thought there was less chance of her trying to strike up a conversation with him than if she had been an adult. He spoke English, but that would not get him very far if anyone on the train was a collaborator.

Once they were out of the Ardennes he might be safe, unless the Germans advanced even further south.

The little girl spoke, startling him. As she spoke in French, he had no idea what she said, but when he looked at her, the meaning was clear. She had opened her satchel and taken out some bread and cheese, both of which she broke in half. She was offering him food. Experience had made him suspicious, so he ignored her at first.

As if she understood his reluctance, she reached over and put the food on the seat beside him, before tucking into her own. He murmured, '*Merci*,' which was the only French he knew, and even then he did not think he pronounced it correctly. It was all he could do not to eat the food ravenously, but he knew that would give him away. So despite the pain in his belly, he ate slowly.

'Do you speak English?' she whispered in that language, looking around just in case anyone stood nearby.

'Yes,' he said.

'You are not French?'

'No.'

She moved seats and sat next to him. Instinctively, Janek moved back. He had become wary of human contact. 'Are you a German?'

'No.'

'I won't tell on you, I promise. I'm on the run too. My name is Anna.' She spoke English without any trace of an accent.

'Janek,' he said under his breath, pronouncing it 'Yanek'. He swallowed the last piece of cheese, wishing he could eat it all over again. When Anna held out her remaining food to him, he shook his head, despite his tummy groaning in disagreement. 'Who are you running from, Anna?'

She ignored his question. 'It's all right, Janek. I'm not very hungry.'

He felt ashamed that it didn't take much persuasion for him to eat the rest of her food.

'Mama is dead now, and my step-father does not want me,' Anna told him. 'So I am going to my father in England. He is a lord. Or a knight. I forget which, but before she died mama told me where to find him. She was a Russian ballerina, so he couldn't marry her. I don't really understand why that is. I mean, if people love each other, they should be able to get married no matter what other people say.' Her voice dropped even lower, to a confessional murmur. 'Mama hid some money for me to use to get away. Step-father didn't know about it. I'm afraid he would be angry if he knew. He might accuse me of stealing.'

'You're away from him now, Anna. Don't worry anymore. Besides, it was your money if your mama left it for you.'

She nodded. 'That's true. Your English is very good.'

'My father owned a hotel in Poland and before the Germans invaded, we had a lot of English visitors. I learned from them. I used to very much enjoy talking to them.' He had also made some English friends, and his hope was that when he reached England they might help him somehow.

'Where is your family now?' Anna asked him.

'The Germans took them away.' He did not have to say any more, not even to a child. Everyone in Europe knew about the camps, even if the rest of the world were either ignorant of their existence or chose to ignore them. 'My father gave me money, but most of it has gone on transport. I did not want to leave him but he said that one of us needed to survive, to tell the truth about what happened.' Janek still carried the weight of the guilt he felt on parting from his family.

'I'm sorry.' Anna slipped her little hand in his. The child's sympathy touched him deeply. It had been a long time since anyone had treated him kindly.

'So have you travelled all the way from Russia?' It felt easier to ask her questions than to answer them.

'Oh no. From Germany. I could have gone to Russia, but Mama said that although it's beautiful, it isn't a nice place to live because of the government.'

'You managed to get out of Germany? How?'

'I don't know really. I just did. It was much easier than I thought. Sometimes if I saw a family, I stayed near them, so that guards would think I was with them. And I am very little, as you can see, so I was often able to lose myself in crowds.'

'You should not be alone, Anna.'

'Mama always said I'm very grown up for my age. I'm ten even though I know I look younger. And you're not that much older than me, yet you're alone.'

Janek supposed he must look younger, given that there was very little meat on his bones nowadays. 'I am eighteen. Old enough to take care of myself. I am going to England to join the Polish forces there, so I can fight for my country.'

'Perhaps we could take care of each other. Until we get to England. I have some money for food and to pay for a boat.' There was something pathetically hopeful about the way she spoke, and a slight tremor entered her voice. Despite her bravado, she was very much a child, all alone in the world.

Janek shook his head. 'I travel alone, Anna. I cannot be responsible for anyone else. Certainly not a child.'

'Do you have any younger brothers and sisters?'

'I had a younger brother, yes. But he died several years ago. I see now it was a blessing.'

'If he hadn't died would you have escaped with him? Or left him behind?'

Janek did not know how to answer that question. 'I am grateful for the food, but do not look to me to be your saviour.' He grieved for the boy he had become. A year or two before, he would not even have considered leaving a child in distress, family or not. But since he had escaped, he had thought

7

only of how he could keep moving and not be slowed down in his quest to reach freedom.

Anna moved back to her own side of the carriage, and once again stared out of the window. He could see the beginnings of tears in her eyes and sensed how hard she was fighting to hide them from him. He felt like every kind of monster, abandoning her, but she would possibly be safer alone than with him. As a child she could blend in with the crowd, in the ways she said. With him, looking the way he did, they would both stand out more.

The guard came along for the tickets. Janek was familiar with the command to see tickets, but was not prepared when the guard fired more questions at him in rapid French. As he stared aghast, afraid that he would be exposed at any moment, Anna started talking to the guard in equally rapid, perfectly accented French, her eyes flashing angrily. Had she betrayed him? Only then did it occur to Janek that she might be a young collaborator. There had been plenty in Poland, children forced into it by fear and hunger. Or perhaps she was angry with him for not helping her to reach England and was getting her revenge that way. The moments that she spoke to the guard seemed to last for an epoch.

When the guard shrugged and left the carriage, Janek waited for him to return with the police.

'Don't worry,' said Anna, pushing the door shut before sitting back down. 'I've told him that you're my servant and that you're deaf and dumb, so can't answer him.'

'And he believed you?'

'Yes, of course. I'm sorry to say that you look like a peasant at the moment, and you were staring at him rather dumbly. Besides, no one would expect a well brought up child like me to travel alone.' She paused for a beat. 'But you don't owe me anything for doing it.'

'Anna, believe it or not, you are probably safer alone.'

'Yes. You're right. I am. We'll say no more of it.'

'Thank you. For the food and for not betraying me.'

It was some time later when Janek noticed a change in the speed of the train. It was going faster; and when they reached a junction, instead of going straight on, as it should have done, it moved onto another track. 'They are diverting the train,' he said.

Anna, who had been dozing, opened her eyes. 'Why are they doing that? Do you think the guard didn't believe my story?' she asked.

'They would not divert a train for one escaped Pole. They would just have police waiting at the station. I think . . . I think the brakes have gone.'

Outside, the train screeched along the track. 'Anna, get onto the floor, quickly.' Janek caught her arm and pulled her down, throwing himself over her as the train finally made contact with something — perhaps a buffer on that line — and the carriages started to buckle and bend, sliding from the track as metal hit metal, and the frightened screams of the passengers could be heard above it all.

When Janek finally got outside, having climbed out through the carriage window, he saw that some of the carriages had rolled over. People were yelling and crying. He knew he should run. In a short time the area would be teeming with the authorities. He climbed down the embankment and was halfway across the field when he remembered Anna. He had left her in the carriage. What would happen to her if the guards found out she was alone? Everything inside him cried out that she was not his responsibility. He had his own life to save, so that he could fight for his country.

But what if she was hurt? Or worse still, what if they sent her to the camps? She was not a Jew or a Pole, but she was Anglo-Russian. Russia had not yet declared war on Germany, but England had. He was not sure what happened to

English prisoners of war, or whether her German step-father could save her. Assuming he even tried. All Janek knew was that if he left her to her fate, he would be seeing her face every time he closed his eyes. He could not become that person, no matter how much his brain told him he should be. His heart disagreed, telling him that if he left a child to suffer, he would live with the guilt the rest of his life. Nothing he did after that time would mean anything, no matter how bravely he fought the war.

He turned and ran back to the train, where everything was still in chaos. At first he lost his bearings, unsure which window he had climbed down from. Then he saw her, sitting on the embankment, sobbing quietly, looking even younger than ever. People rushed around her, but not one person stopped to help.

Someone had to take care of her, and whilst all his common sense told him to leave her there, his conscience would not allow it. He had seen many unpleasant things since leaving Poland. He would not give himself entirely up to the horror by abandoning a little girl who had shown him kindness. Perhaps by saving her he could salvage something of the boy he used to be.

'Anna!' He rushed to her and held out his hand, which she took gratefully. 'It is all right, little one. Come with me. I will take care of you.'

2

'I think this is the place,' said Anna. They had arrived in southern England the night before, sleeping in the station waiting room before getting the train to Surrey. Although exhausted, they still had to walk some five miles from the local station. Anna had very little money left, so they were both very tired and very hungry. 'My father is Sir Lionel Silverton, and this is Silverton Hall.'

It was certainly impressive — a Georgian manor in the leafiest part of Surrey. Janek had read about such places from his English friends, but had never seen them. He wished he had time to admire it, but there were more important things to do.

'I will leave you here,' said Janek when they reached the gatehouse. 'I must get to London.'

'No!' Anna grabbed his arm. 'Please come in with me and help me explain, Janek. I won't know what to say.'

'You always know what to say, Anna. You are better at being on the run than I am. You speak Russian, French and English, whereas I speak only Polish and not very good English.'

'Please . . . '

'I will come to the door, but I cannot stay. We agreed, remember?'

'Yes, I know,' she said glumly. 'We go as far as England together, then separate. I wish we didn't have to though. You're the only friend I have.'

'That will change when you meet your father.' Janek was not as certain of that as he pretended. It was only as they neared the front door that he began to question if Sir Lionel even knew he had a daughter. What if Anna's mother had lied? Anna's real father might be someone else entirely. It would leave the child in an impossible situation. Then she might become his responsibility. But that would not happen. He was sure there were societies and other places in Britain that looked after children. He would help her to find one of those.

They approached the house hand-in-hand, Janek becoming acutely aware of how shabby they must both look. Anna had been forced to leave her suitcase behind on the crashed train, and he only had the clothes in which he stood.

A homely-looking woman in her thirties answered the door. She introduced herself as Mrs Palmer.

'I am Anna, Sir Lionel's daughter. And this is my friend, Janek.'

'Sir Lionel's daughter? Not the little Russian girl?' said Mrs. Palmer. Her face broke into a warm-hearted smile. 'Well, I never. I met your mother when she came to London to dance. You are just as pretty as she is, with that lovely black hair and those blue eyes. And she had wonderful cheekbones. I'm sure you'll get those as you get older.' Mrs. Palmer paused for breath. 'Oh, listen to me prattling on; and you'll want to be seeing your father, won't you? I'll go and tell Sir Lionel.'

Janek guessed he was not the only one breathing a sigh of relief. At least Anna's parentage was not in question.

Five minutes later, Sir Lionel came to the hall, accompanied by a young woman in her late twenties. She was rather over-blown looking, with peroxide-blonde hair and blood-red lipstick. At first Janek thought she must be another daughter.

'I am Sir Lionel Silverton and this is my wife, Geraldine. Who did you say you were?' Sir Lionel looked them both up and down, with distaste in his eyes.

'I'm your daughter, Anna.'

'Natalia's girl? Well, this is a turn up for the books.' His welcome was nowhere near as warm as Mrs Palmer's, but at least he was not unfriendly. 'Where is your mother?'

'She's dead . . . sir . . . ' Anna clutched Janek's hand, and he under-stood she was overwhelmed by the grandness of the house and of the man standing before her. 'I escaped from

Germany, with my friend Janek. He saved me from a train crash. May I stay with you?'

Sir Lionel looked a little taken aback. He turned to his wife, who Janek saw imperceptibly shake her head. He wondered if Anna had noticed. Probably. She was a perceptive child, and easily picked up on the subtle nuances of body language. Her hand gripping his tighter still told him that she had seen it.

'I'm afraid that's impossible,' said Sir Lionel. 'As I've told you, Anna, I'm married now, and to be frank, your appearance here is rather uncomfortable. I'm afraid you and your friend Janek will have to go elsewhere. There's no one to take responsibility for you here. I'll give you both some money . . . '

'Just one minute.' Janek stepped forward, speaking angrily. It was not just so that he could free himself of responsibility to Anna. If he had to keep taking care of her, so be it. But he would do his best to ensure this man understood his obligations first. 'I want nothing from you, sir. But Anna, she is your daughter. Your responsibility. And I will not leave here until I have your assurance that she has somewhere safe to live.'

'We don't want her,' said Geraldine, speaking for the first time. 'Take her away.'

'I'll take responsibility for her, sir.' No one had seen Mrs Palmer come back to the hallway. 'Excuse me for speaking out of turn, sir. It wouldn't be right to leave the poor little thing to fend for herself during wartime. Not after her mother meant so much to you.' Mrs Palmer glanced at Geraldine defiantly, clearly reminding Sir Lionel's wife of things she would rather forget. 'Don't worry; I'll keep her out of your and Lady Silverton's way.'

'Yes,' said Geraldine. 'Bring her up with the servants.'

'She is not a servant,' said Janek. 'She is a well-brought up, intelligent young lady, and she should be treated as such.'

'It's all right, Janek,' said Anna. She looked up at him with tearstained eyes. 'I'll stay with Mrs Palmer. I like her better anyway.' She turned to her father. 'Janek needs money to get to London. And for food.'

'Anna . . . ' Janek protested. Over the weeks they had travelled together, her directness had amused him. Now it embarrassed him, even though he knew she meant well.

'Yes, you do. I'd be dead if not for you.'

Looking around the hall, Janek had the sad impression that for at least two people there, that would not have been such a bad thing. He hated leaving her in this place, but he was heartened by believing that the doughty Mrs Palmer would fight for her.

'I'll give you five pounds,' said Sir Lionel. 'That should be enough. What are your plans?'

'I intend to join the Polish forces in Britain, sir, and fight for my country.'

'Good man. Mrs Palmer, why don't

you give, erm . . . ?'

'Janek,' said Anna. 'Janek Dabrowski.'

'Yes, Mr Dabrowski. Give him some food before he leaves.'

'Is that really necessary, Lionel?' said Geraldine, folding her arms and tapping her foot on the floor. 'You're giving him money and food, when all he's brought us is trouble.'

'Despite what you think, Geraldine,' said Sir Lionel through gritted teeth, 'I still like to believe I'm master in my own house.'

'Of course, darling. Of course. I'm sorry; I didn't mean to be such a grouch. It's just that when you told me about her I didn't expect we'd have to bring her up.'

Sir Lionel did not answer. He walked away without saying a word to anyone.

An hour later, Janek was walking down the drive with money in his pocket and some food that Mrs Palmer had insisted on packing for him. 'Don't worry, dear,' she had said. 'I know a man who can get butter and cheese on the black market.

Sir Lionel doesn't mind as long as his table is well-stocked.'

'Janek!' Anna ran after him, and when he turned, she flung herself into his arms. 'Please don't forget me, Janek.'

'I won't forget you. Hey, you saved my life.'

'Promise me that when the war is over, you'll come back. We can live as brother and sister. Say you will, Janek. You're my only friend.'

'Yes, I'll come back and we can be brother and sister.'

'I love you, Janek.'

'Take care, little one.'

He had believed it would be very easy to relinquish responsibility for her. After all, he had only saved her to salve his own conscience, and he could tell himself without a stain on his conscience he had succeeded in that aim. But as he walked away, leaving her in a home where she would not be loved or appreciated, and knowing that he had lied about returning for her one day, he felt a lump in his throat and tears stinging his eyes.

3

'And when you've finished changing the beds, Anna, would you mind dusting the furniture in your father's . . . in Sir Lionel's study?'

'Of course, Mrs Palmer,' said Anna. It had long been impressed upon both of them that neither Anna nor anyone else in the house was to refer to Sir Lionel as Anna's father. But Mrs Palmer clung to her belief that Sir Lionel should properly recognise his daughter, so was apt to slip up from time to time.

'I hate asking you to do these things,' said Mrs Palmer. 'It's not right that the daughter of a knight should be expected to clean rooms and live in servant's quarters.'

Anna smiled. It was a regular refrain and had been for the eight years she had lived at Silverton Hall. 'I don't mind,' she said. 'It keeps me busy, and I like helping you after all you've done for me.'

'Oh, I've done nothing. At least, not more than a real Christian would do in the circumstances. Not that there's much Christian charity around this house.' She sniffed loudly. She spoke more gently. 'You're a good girl. It would make my heart happy to see you sitting properly at your father's table, being courted by handsome young noblemen.'

The eight years had seen Anna grow from a scrawny child into a very pretty young woman. It had also seen the end of the war. 'I'm not interested in noblemen, handsome or otherwise.'

'Oh, you're not still hoping for young Janek to return are you, dear?'

Anna smiled. 'No, I got over that a long time ago. He lied to me. But I think he did it for the right reasons. I was not his responsibility and he had other more important things to do. Did you see that he won a medal for bravery?'

'Yes, I saw it the last dozen times you showed me the piece in the paper,' said Mrs Palmer, patting Anna on the shoulder.

Anna sat down on the edge of the bed. Any of the other housemaids doing such a thing would have heard the sharp edge of Mrs Palmer's tongue, but not Anna. Besides, Mrs Palmer knew that Anna worked harder than any of them. It was as if she felt the need to prove something. 'I just wish he'd replied to my letters,' she said, becoming glum. The only time she ever looked unhappy was when she thought of Janek. She could easily ignore the daily insults from her step-mother and the indifference from her father. But Janek refusing to even answer her letters was painful to her, even if she did understand that all they were to each other was two children who had shared a terrifying experience a long time ago.

'I'm pretty sure that flying around in

the sky, giving Hitler what-for, didn't give him much time for letter-writing,' said Mrs Palmer. 'Now come on, these beds won't make themselves.'

Anna knew that Mrs Palmer did not mean it unkindly. She just hated to see Anna upset. 'I'm glad I've got you,' she said to the housekeeper, kissing her on the cheek.

'Oh, go away with you girl. I haven't got time for sloppy stuff.' Nevertheless, when Mrs Palmer left the room, she secretly wiped a tear from her eye.

Anna continued with her work, and as she had every day for eight years, she wondered what Janek was doing. Had he returned to Poland? Or did he live in Britain? It was possible he had found a nice girl to marry. Anna felt no jealousy on that score. She thought of Janek more as a friend or older brother. If he had married, she thought she would rather like to be aunty to his children, on account of him not having any other family left. Being a part of Janek's family was an idle fantasy that she often conjured up to get herself through the days of living as an outsider in her real family's home.

When she had finished the bed-rooms, she went downstairs and started dusting her father's study, first ensuring he was not in there. He did not like to be disturbed whilst working, although once or twice when Anna had inadvertently disturbed him, it seemed that he only stared into space. The study was out of bounds to everyone, so she wondered if Sir Lionel went there to escape rather than to work.

'Anna!' A young fair-haired boy of about eight came bounding down the stairs and through the study door.

'Morning, Teddy. How are you this morning?'

'I'm very well, thank you, Anna. I've got a new airplane.' Teddy Silverton, Anna's half-brother, waved a toy plane in the air. 'I'm just about to go and bomb a city somewhere. Which city shall I bomb?'

'Oh dear, that won't be very nice for

the people living there, will it? Why don't you just fly over the city and marvel at the sights? I hear that cities look lovely from the air, especially at night with all the lights on.'

'That's boring, Anna. You're no fun.'

'That's because I'm rather busy, Teddy. I don't really have time to plan bombing raids.' Anna had dusted the bookshelves, and moved on to the desk.

'Well, will you try and make time later? I've no one else to play with and Mama doesn't mind you playing with me as she says it keeps me quiet.'

'Very well, Teddy. I'll play with you in the garden after lunch if the weather is fine. But only if Mrs Palmer can spare me.'

'I'll go and ask her now. She has to do anything I tell her to, because I am the son and heir.'

'Teddy!'

'What?' Teddy looked bemused. 'That's what Mama says.'

'I'm sure she does,' said Anna, tight-lipped. 'Whilst it's true that Mrs

Palmer is a servant, that does not mean that you can treat her unkindly or unfairly. She is still a person, Teddy.'

'She's a very old person.'

Anna laughed. 'No, I think she's about fifty. That's not very old. It's younger than Papa . . . I mean younger than your Papa.' She had no idea how much Teddy knew about who she really was. It was something Geraldine did not like mentioned in front of her son.

'It's all right, Anna; I know you're my half-sister. I heard Mama arguing with Papa about it. I promise that as I have a sister who is a servant, I shall be very nice to all servants in future.'

Anna wanted to hug the child, but dared not. 'That's a very good way to behave, Teddy. I think you'll make a very good son and heir.'

'I hope so.' Teddy became glum. 'It seems rather a lot of fuss. Papa tried to tell me the other day how I must look after the estate. He showed me rows and rows of numbers. Anna . . . '

'What is it, dear?'

'I'm not terribly good at sums, and there were an awful lot of them. What if I can't do it properly?'

'Well,' said Anna, walking over to him and putting her hands on his shoulders, 'since you don't have to start work on the estate immediately, and probably have at least another ten years before you do, I shouldn't worry about it. Now go on out in the garden to play so I can get on with my work.'

'You're a peach,' said Teddy, reaching up and kissing her cheek. 'When I'm in charge, I shall let you be a proper lady and find you a prince or lord to marry.'

'I wish people would stop trying to fix me up with nobility,' said Anna, laughing.

Teddy ran out into the hall. As Anna followed his progress to the front door, she saw her step-mother standing nearby, glaring at her.

Geraldine walked into the study, slamming the door behind her. 'You need not think that by getting yourself into Edward's good graces that you can change your position here,' she said haughtily. 'You are not fit for anything other than the servant's hall.'

'I understand that,' said Anna, determined not to be browbeaten. 'Teddy . . . '

'Master Edward to you.'

'I apologise. Master Edward was only being kind. He's just a little boy, and doesn't mean half of what he says.'

'As long as you know that. Be aware that as soon as your father dies, you will not continue to live in this house. It is an outrage that you do live here, reminding me of your father's relation-ship with that . . . that . . . '

'Whatever happened between my mother and father happened before he met you,' said Anna. 'It is not their fault that the snobbish values in this country prevented them from marrying when they were in love.'

'How dare you speak to me like that? I know what you're about, sneaking around your father's study so that you can find out if he's made provision for you in his will. Well I can tell you now that he has not, so you're wasting your time.'

Anna was infuriated by the injustice in Geraldine's words. She had no interest in inheriting from her father. The only reason she stayed on at Silverton Hall was because she had nowhere else to go. 'I am not snooping,' she said, clenching her hands into a fist to try and stem the growing anger and despair.

If Geraldine believed she was and passed on that gossip to Sir Lionel, Anna might well find herself out on the street. Not for the first time in the eight years since she had come to Silverton Hall did she ponder on how fragile her place was in this house.

'Go on, back upstairs,' said Geraldine. 'I shall speak to Mrs Palmer and tell her that in future you are to keep to the kitchen and the upstairs rooms. I don't want you in the public rooms or the private family apartments.' She emphasised the word 'family' to let

Anna know that she was most certainly not counted amongst that group of people.

'I haven't finished . . . ' Anna started to say.

'You have finished! Now go!'

4

Anna wiped her eyes with a hankie as Mrs. Palmer put a cup of tea in front of her. 'There now, child, don't take on so,' she said gently. 'Oh, that woman . . . There's been nothing but trouble since she came to this house. You might think she'll throw you out, dear, but I know she won't. So many servants have come and gone since she married your father. She doesn't know how to treat them. In the old days, servants didn't have much choice, but since the war young girls can have different careers in shops and offices, and that's what they want. Who's going to clean up after others, and work till past midnight having to get up again at six, when there are better paid jobs out there where you can be home by five o'clock and in bed by ten? I'd go myself. I've often had dreams of running a guest house by the sea, but . . . '

'What?' Anna looked up at her, teary-eyed. 'Oh, Mrs Palmer, please don't say you're only staying because of me? I'd feel awful.'

'Then you mustn't. I promised that lad and God I'd take care of you, and take care of you I will. As long as I'm here, no harm will come to you.'

Anna sipped her tea, feeling humbled by Mrs Palmer's sacrifice. It was not fair that the housekeeper carried on working somewhere she was clearly miserable because of Anna. 'Mrs Palmer,' she said quietly a few minutes later.

Mrs Palmer was peeling potatoes. It was not her job, but the cook had quit the week before, and the kitchen maid the week before that. The other staff were stretched to the limit with the demands that Lady Silverton made of them. 'What, dear?'

'You said you'd quite like to run a guesthouse?'

'Ay, it's an idle dream, but my sister's

husband left her a bit of money in his will. Did I tell you?'

'Yes, you did.'

'Well, me and our Elsie thought we'd run a guesthouse together. It's something we talk about in our letters. She works as a cook for the Duke of Northumberland, you know. I suppose it helps us to dream a little. Makes the days go a bit quicker.'

'Oh.'

'What? Do you not think it's a good idea?'

'Oh yes, it's a wonderful idea. It's just that I was going to suggest I come and help you. Then we could both leave here.'

Mrs Palmer turned around and smiled. 'Now why didn't I think of that? I'll write and ask our Elsie what she thinks, but I'm sure she won't mind. You could be a chambermaid. Not that we'd be able to pay you much.'

'I don't mind, honestly. As long as it's away from here.'

'I know you don't, dear. But I do.

Oh, it pains me . . . ' Mrs Palmer once again bemoaned the way Anna was treated by her father and mistreated by her step-mother. She had heard it all before, and she knew it came from a place of affection. But complaining about it did not change things.

'I'd better go and play with Teddy,' said Anna. 'I did promise.' Careful to keep out of the main gardens, Anna spent a happy hour playing with her half-brother near the vegetable patch. It was a place she knew her step-mother would never venture.

The patch looked forlorn in the afternoon sunlight. Since the last gardener — the latest in a long line — had left in a huff, Anna, Mrs Palmer and Mr Stephens the butler had done their best to keep it maintained, but it was difficult to do when they had so many other duties. Yet with certain things still being rationed, it was their only way of putting fresh vegetables on the table.

'I want to climb that tree,' said

Teddy, pointing to an apple tree.

'Oh no, Teddy, I don't think you should,' said Anna. She was afraid of what her step-mother might say if Teddy fell and hurt himself.

'Aw, Anna, other boys climb trees. They laugh at me at school because I won't. I thought that if I practise at home, I'll be good by the time I go back to boarding school.'

'You'd best ask your mama and papa first,' said Anna. 'Then maybe you can do it another day. I don't want to get into any trouble.'

'All right,' said Teddy, pouting. Being a child of generally good spirits, he soon cheered up and they ran around the vegetable patch with their arms outstretched, pretending to be airplanes. Later he helped Anna collect windblown apples.

'We can have apple crumble for tea,' she promised him.

'Yummy. With custard?' He bit into one of the apples.

'With custard. Although you won't be

very hungry if you eat them all first.'

'An apple a day keeps the doctor away,' said Teddy. 'Anna?'

'What is it, dear?'

'I'd rather like to be a doctor.'

'Would you?'

'Yes. I've been reading about it. Mother says I can't because I'm a gentleman and gentlemen don't work. But I think that's rather silly. Mind you, I would have to get better at arithmetic.'

'I'll help you, if you like,' Anna promised.

'You're a peach of a girl,' said Teddy.

For the next few days, rather than dreaming of joining Janek's family, Anna had a new dream. One of going to work in a bed and breakfast by the seaside. She and Mrs Palmer talked about it whilst they worked and late into the night, when they could not sleep for excitement. Mrs Palmer's sister, Elsie Smith, had agreed that Anna could join them as a chambermaid.

'It'll be nothing too big,' said Mrs Palmer over cocoa one night. 'Just a few rooms, so we're not run off our feet. After all, what's the point of living by the seaside if you can't sometimes go and walk along the sands?'

'Have you thought of where?' asked Anna.

'Yes, we thought up Filey way, or Scarborough. We used to go there as children. Oh, it's lovely up there.'

'I'd love to travel more,' said Anna dreamily. To say how much of her young life had been spent travelling from one country to another, she had very little recollection of it, after eight years of only ever being at Silverton Hall. The other servants, in the days when they had a full staff, would go to the seaside on their days off. As Anna was not actually paid a wage, she could never afford to join them. Mrs Palmer had offered her the money to go, but she always refused, feeling she had taken enough of the kind lady's charity. Her clothes were generally hand-me-downs, courtesy of other maids who also took kindly to her.

'You'll be travelling to the east coast with us, dear,' said Mrs Palmer. 'And you needn't think we'll use you as a drudge either. I've warned our Elsie about that. I've told her about how you're a proper little Cinderella here, and she agrees with me that you deserve to be treated better.'

Anna reached out and put her hand over Mrs Palmer's. 'I know you'll be kind to me. You always have been.'

'And always will be. You've got a friend in Polly Palmer and don't you ever forget that.'

Anna did forget it, and only a few days later at that.

5

Anna had been busy all morning, on account of yet another servant leaving. Mrs Palmer had put a postcard in the local shop and asked a London agency to send someone quickly, but the truth was that Geraldine Silverton's behaviour was becoming well known.

'It's amazing,' said Mrs Palmer as she scrubbed the kitchen table with salt whilst Anna was busy in the pantry, washing the breakfast dishes. They talked through the open door. 'Servants have to give references when they want a job, when really it's employers who should have to give them.'

'What are we going to do?' said Anna. 'There's only me, you and Mr Stephens the butler now, and he's retiring soon.'

'It won't be our problem in a little while, child. We'll be off. Elsie has seen a property she likes, and is going to put in an offer on it.'

'That will be wonderful.' Anna smiled. 'But poor Mr Stephens.'

'Don't worry about him. I've told him he can retire to our guest house. Mind you, don't go telling the council. There's a residency by-law of twenty-eight days in most places. But if you can't help an old friend, who can you help? He'd only have to go to his sister, and they don't get on very well. That's the trouble with this job. It takes your whole life from you, then spits you out when you're no use anymore.'

Although Mrs Palmer was prone to moaning a little, Anna had never heard her sound so bitter and discontented. She supposed it was because in the housekeeper's mind, she was already running the guesthouse. Even for Anna, every day at Silverton Hall seemed to drag more than ever. 'Have you handed in your notice?' she asked.

'Yes. The new housekeeper will be arriving in a month. Have you?'

'For what reason?' asked Anna. 'I'm not really employed. In fact . . . could we not say that I'm going until the day we leave? I don't doubt my father and step-mother will be glad to get rid of me, but I'm still afraid there will be bad feeling.' In reality, Anna was terrified that with no servants to run the place, her father and step-mother might actually force her to stay to cook and clean for them.

'This is exactly why I didn't say anything when I handed in my notice. I don't want you stuck here doing everything,' said Mrs Palmer, as if she had read Anna's mind. 'But, whilst I hate to say this, dear, I don't think your step-mother will be sorry to see you go. I think I know the real reason she doesn't want you at the front of the house. It's because you've grown into such a pretty girl. She's like the wicked witch in 'Snow White'. She doesn't want the competition.'

Anna could not help laughing, but was also concerned. 'Please be careful,

Mrs Palmer. If she ever hears you . . . '

'Oh, what can she do? I'm already leaving and our Elsie won't see us out on the street until we get the guesthouse up and running.'

'Even so, do be careful.' Anna felt a sudden shiver down her spine as if someone had walked over her grave and a cloud passed across the sun. She supposed that like Mrs Palmer, she was eager to be gone from Silverton Hall, so her fears that it might not happen, or was not happening soon enough, were overwhelming her. 'I'm afraid that even if she can't hurt you here, she may do something to harm your chances of running the guesthouse.'

'Goodness, child, she isn't that powerful.'

'I know, but . . . '

'You're right of course, and my old mother used to say that if you can't say anything nice about someone you shouldn't say anything at all. So that's the last thing you'll hear me say on the subject.' Mrs Palmer paused for a beat.

'Just don't go accepting any shiny apples from her.'

Anna giggled and stacked the last of the plates up. 'What are we cooking tonight? I'll go and get the vegetables.'

'With Sir Lionel up at his club in London, there's only your step-mother and Master Teddy to worry about. I'll do him the chicken, and there's a piece of steak in the larder for your step-mother. I gather she's dining alone tonight. Just as well, as the ration cards only go so far and she expects miracles. The steak is something the butcher got for me, no questions asked.' Mrs. Palmer tapped her nose. 'We look after him with vegetables. Or, we did when we had more. So hopefully that will keep her happy. I'll be glad when this rationing is finished with. I don't understand it. You'd think now the war was over, we'd be getting proper food again instead of all this austerity. And we're supposed to have won at that.' She stopped scrubbing and paused to think. 'Me, you and Mr Stephens will have that broth left over from yesterday's lunch. We can bulk it up with a few more potatoes, I suppose.'

'Very well. I shan't be a minute.'

'I'm off to the village as soon as I've finished this,' said Mrs Palmer. 'So don't worry if I'm not here when you get back. Perhaps you could start peeling the potatoes and carrots.'

When Anna reached the vegetable patch, Teddy was there, pretending to fly his plane over the carrots. 'Pow pow pow!' he cried. 'Take that, you evil carrots.' Anna recognised a boy who was ready to be back at school. She felt the familiar pang that she had not been allowed the same chance. She had read as much as she could, when she was able — not permitted to use her father's books, she relied on the local library, but it was not the same as structured teaching. She felt that she was very ignorant about many things. It was the reason she also felt that, unlike other girls, she could not go out and get a different job.

Anna laughed. 'They're not evil, Teddy.'

'Oh yes they are. And so are sprouts.'

'Hmm. I see. I suppose that's because you don't like eating them.'

'Too true.'

'But they're very good for you.'

'They don't taste good. Not like ice cream.'

'I'll agree with you there.'

'I'd like to eat ice cream all the time,' said Teddy.

'You'd soon get bored with it and long for carrots and sprouts,' Anna teased.

'Anna . . . '

'Hmm?'

'I asked Mama and Papa about climbing the tree and they said it was all right as long as you were here. Shall I do it now?'

'Well I'm very busy at the moment, Teddy. Perhaps later.' She kneeled down and started pulling some carrots from the ground.

Teddy was not listening. He was

already putting his small feet on a large knot on the tree trunk and hauling himself up.

'Teddy . . . ' Anna once again felt as if someone walked over her grave. 'No, please don't, Teddy.'

'It's easy-peasy,' he called from halfway up. 'Look, Anna, the boys at school won't laugh at me again.'

'Teddy, please come down.' Why Anna felt so much dread, she did not know. Little boys climbed trees and scraped their knees all the time. But Teddy had been mollycoddled by his mother, and was never allowed to do any of those things. Only then did Anna realise that he had lied to her about getting permission. She felt a little bit angry with him, but reminded herself that he was only a little boy after all. 'Dearest, please don't climb so high. You've proved your point, and I'm sure the other boys won't laugh at you anymore.'

'Oh, but I want to sit on the top branch,' said Teddy.

'I don't think you should do that!' Anna was alarmed. She dropped the carrots she had picked onto the earth and went over to the tree. 'Teddy, I am asking you nicely, dear, not to go any higher. Come down.'

'Look, Anna, I'm on top of the world. Like Jimmy Cagney.' Teddy had reached the middle branches. He lifted his foot in an attempt to get a grip on the next branch. That was when all Anna's fears came to fruition. He stepped up badly and lost his footing, falling to the ground with a sickening thud.

'Teddy!' Anna screamed. He lay on the ground with his eyes closed, groaning quietly. She knelt down and touched his head. He felt clammy and hot. 'Teddy, dearest, please speak to me.' He did not answer her. He just opened his eyes drowsily.

Anna jumped up and ran back to the kitchen, calling for Mrs Palmer. 'She's gone off to the town on the morning bus, lass,' said Mr Stephens, who had come into the kitchen for his morning coffee.

'It's Teddy,' Anna said breathlessly. 'He's fallen from the tree. I think he's badly hurt.'

'I'll go and fetch the mistress,' said Mr Stephens, scraping his chair back hurriedly.

It never occurred to Anna at that moment that Teddy's fall would be seen as anything other than an unfortunate accident. She was too busy worrying if he was badly hurt. She went back to the garden and cradled his head in her arms. 'Where does it hurt, Teddy?' she asked.

'My leg . . . and my head,' Teddy said, with tears coming from his eyes.

Seconds later, Geraldine Silverton came running from the house, crying, 'My baby boy, my baby boy! Stephens, call the doctor immediately.' She reached the base of the tree where Anna sat cradling Teddy and practically spat at Anna, 'What were you doing whilst my son was climbing the tree?'

'Er . . . I was picking vegetables, Lady Silverton.'

'Picking vegetables whilst my son was getting into danger. Teddy, why on earth did you climb the tree? You silly boy.' Despite her hysterical behaviour, Geraldine made no attempt to touch Teddy herself. It was almost as if she was afraid of catching something from him.

'Anna said I could,' said Teddy, looking sheepishly at his half-sister.

'Teddy, that's not true,' said Anna. 'You said . . . ' She was unable to say anything else because Geraldine interrupted her.

'You! You did it on purpose. I know what your game is. You're trying to harm my baby boy so you can take his place as heir to Silverton Hall.'

'No!' Anna exclaimed. 'I would never hurt Teddy. Never.'

'When Stephens comes back, I shall ask him to phone the police. We'll see what you say to them. Now get away from my child and wait in the kitchen.

Attempted murder, that's what it is.'

'But . . . ' Anna was too upset to say anything else. She scrambled up from the ground and staggered to the kitchen. The police would come and arrest her, and they would believe everything her step-mother said.

Mr Stephens was waiting by the back door, having just got off the phone to the doctor. 'I didn't do it,' she said to Stephens.

'I know, lass.' He followed her back into the kitchen. 'What to do, that's the problem. If Polly Palmer were here, she would know.' He reached into his pocket. 'I've only got a ten-shilling note, but it should get you on the bus to town. Go and find her, and ask her to help.'

'What about my step-mother?'

'I'll hold her off. I'll tell her you've gone to your room. Go on, lass. Polly will know what to do. She always does.'

Anna left the house by the front door, knowing that her step-mother was at the back with Teddy. The doctor passed in his car just as she reached the gatehouse. Used to seeing Anna around, he nodded to her politely, but did not stop. No one dallied when Geraldine Silverton summoned them.

Unable to wait for the next bus because her nerves were so ragged, Anna started to walk the five miles to the town. If a bus passed by she would flag it down, but she could not wait by the roadside.

Walking gave her time to think about the problem. How could she ever convince her step-mother that she had not tried to harm Teddy? The more she thought about it, the more she began to realise that her step-mother thought no such thing. It was just an excuse to get Anna into trouble. The police would listen to Geraldine, too. Anna had no friends, apart from Mrs Palmer and Mr Stephens. No one else would stick up for her. And as kind as they both were, they were only servants. They had as few rights as she did.

And what if Mrs Palmer believed

Geraldine? She would not want Anna to join her at the guesthouse then. That was assuming Anna had not been carted off to prison first. Unsure of English law, because her life at Silverton Hall had been so sheltered, Anna feared it might even affect Mrs Palmer's chances of owning a guesthouse if it was known she fraternised with a convicted felon.

By the time she was halfway to the town, she knew that she could not involve her dearest friend in this scandal. Neither could she return to Silverton Hall. All she owned was there, such as it was, but she dare not go back and collect it first.

At the town, Anna did her best to keep out of sight. If Mrs Palmer saw her she would surely wonder why she was there. She prayed she would not bump into anyone else she knew. Not that there were many people.

Making her way to the station, Anna bought a ticket to London, using the ten-shilling note that Mr Stephens had given her. She waited on a bench on the platform, aware that she had once again stolen from someone in order to escape. This time with less reason. She was no longer a child escaping the Nazis. She was a teenaged girl on the run from the police. With a sob, she put her head in her hands.

6

Janek Dabrowski unlocked the door with a feeling of deep satisfaction. It was his at last! He pushed the door open and stepped inside.

Streams of refracted light fell from the cracks in the curtains, revealing dusty tables and armchairs. The floor was in need of a deep polish, and the foyer would need a new reception desk, what with the old one having been destroyed during a bombing raid.

Admittedly it needed a bit of work, but he was not afraid of that. 'I don't know how to thank you for your help, Mike,' he said to his friend, Michael Carmichael, who followed him in. Mike was a cheerful Scot, with the red hair to match.

'You're welcome, Jan,' said Mike. 'With your knowledge of running a hotel, and my knowledge of living in them for most of my life whilst dear old Pa was in the diplomatic service, we'll make a good team. Are you sure you don't mind it being called Carmichael's?'

'Not at all. Given the mistrust of foreigners in Britain since the war, I think that's the best option, don't you? Otherwise we'll never fill the place.' Over the years, Janek's Polish accent had faded. It was still there, in the way he pronounced certain words, but one had to listen for it. He also looked very different from when Anna had last seen him. Decent food and a reasonably good life since nineteen forty had helped him fill out a little. He had also grown by several inches, reaching over six feet in height. Only his friends noticed that sometimes, when Janek did not think he was being observed, his face was beset by a haunted look.

'Except that you were one of our biggest heroes,' said Mike.

'I don't think that counts for much.'

'Don't be so hard on yourself. So,

when do we open this place?'

'As soon as possible. Come on, let's find some brooms.'

'Hey,' Mike laughed, 'when I said I'd be a sleeping partner, I meant it entirely. I'm going to sleep whilst you do all the hard work.'

'No chance,' said Jan, laughing. 'Come on, you spoiled Scot. I'm going to teach you the meaning of hard work.'

'Hey,' said Mike, half an hour later, whilst they swept the floors. Unfortunately all they seemed to succeed in doing was move the dust around. 'I forgot to tell you. My sister, Mary, says to say hello.'

'Tell Mary hello back,' said Janek curtly.

'Oh come on, Jan. You know she's crazy about you since you came to stay at the castle.'

'She's also very young, Mike. Let the girl grow up a bit before you start trying to marry her off.'

'Mary has been grown up since the age of ten.'

'Hmm.' Janek left it at that, but the mention of Mary at the age often reminded him of Anna. He often wondered how she was doing. No doubt her natural charm had won her father over, and she was now a grand lady. He still had some of her letters, but they mentioned very little of her life at Silverton Hall or what she did there. Janek knew he should have replied, but he had made a decision to break off all contact with Anna, for her sake as much as for his own, and he had been determined to stick to it. Only occasionally did the guilt of that abandonment catch up with him.

'Penny for them,' said Mike.

'I was just thinking of that kid. The one I told you about.'

'Oh yeah. Silverton's girl.' Mike was the only one who really knew how Janek felt about leaving her at Silverton Hall, eight years before. 'I'm sure she's fine, Janek. She wrote to you, didn't she? Put her out of your mind, chum.'

'Do you ever stop and think about

the things we did during the war?' asked Janek, leaning on his broom. 'The things we were forced to do to survive?'

'Sometimes,' said Mike.

'She's my greatest regret. I sometimes wish I could see her, just to make sure she is all right.'

'Well go down to Silverton Hall and ask after her. It's only just south of the river, in Surrey.'

'Yes, perhaps I will one day.' Janek nodded. 'Good idea.' Thinking about doing something positive about Anna seemed to have the effect of pushing her even further to the back of his head.

* * *

When Mrs Palmer returned to Silverton Hall later that day, she found Mr Stephens sitting at the kitchen table.

'Did Anna find you, Polly?' he asked. His face was lined with worry.

'Anna?' Mrs Palmer felt a chill on the back of her neck and immediately realised something was terribly wrong.

'What has happened, Horace?'

'Young Teddy fell from the tree and the mistress decided Anna was trying to get him out of the way.'

'Nonsense! She thinks the world of that little boy.'

'I thought that. So I gave the girl ten shillings and sent her to find you.'

'I haven't seen her. Are you sure she didn't hide in the house somewhere?'

'I don't think so. The doctor saw her going out through the gates.'

When it became clear later that evening that Anna was not going to return, Mrs Palmer was beside herself. 'Who knows where that poor child is,' she said, sniffing into her hankie. 'Out there all alone in the world. Oh, it doesn't bear thinking about. She doesn't know the world like we do, having been locked up here for eight years. Anyone might take advantage of her.'

'I wonder,' said Mr Stephens as he dried the dinner dishes, 'whether I should tell Sir Lionel about the ten-shilling note.'

'Horace Stephens,' said Mrs Palmer, taking him by the shoulders, 'you know as well as I do that my Anna is not a thief! If you so much as breathe a word to Sir Lionel or the mistress about those ten shillings, you can jolly well find somewhere else to live when you retire! Really, Horace, if the ten shillings means that much, I'll give it to you, but you will not blacken that poor girl's name any further.'

'I don't want the money back, Polly. If it's any use to young Anna, then I don't begrudge her a penny of it. I just thought that it might help with finding her. I mean, it's not going to get her very far, is it?'

'Then you're not thinking clearly. You know as well as I do that Lady Geraldine will only use it as another excuse to think badly of Anna.'

'Excuse me,' said a little voice behind them. 'I have ten shillings in my savings, if you would like it back, Mr Stephens.' They turned to see Teddy standing nearby.

'That's perfectly all right, Master Edward,' said Mrs Palmer stiffly. She was not very pleased with young Teddy at that moment. 'We may be servants but we can manage ten shillings for a friend.'

'I'm so sorry,' said Teddy, his eyes brimming with tears. 'I didn't mean . . . I didn't know what Mother was going to say. I've tried to tell her I lied, but she won't listen. Please don't be angry with me, Mrs Palmer.'

Not one who could really be unkind to a child, Mrs Palmer held out motherly arms to him, and he gratefully accepted her embrace. 'Oh, I know, Master Teddy,' she said, stroking his head. 'You're just a little boy and little boys sometimes tell fibs if they think they're in trouble. You didn't mean no harm. It's just that your mother has had it in for your sister since she came here.'

'Perhaps we could go and look for Anna,' Teddy suggested. 'I do have a bit of money. We could hire a private detective.'

'How much money do you have in your savings?' asked Mrs Palmer, smiling.

'About one pound, ten shillings and sixpence.'

'I think a private detective costs a little bit more than that. We'll just have to look for her ourselves.'

Without knowing which direction Anna had taken, that was going to prove to be very difficult indeed.

7

It was mid-afternoon when Anna reached central London. Having got there, she hesitated. What could she do next? She had nowhere to stay, and no job. She managed to buy a penny bun from a stall, but it did little to sate her hunger. With only a couple of shillings left in her pocket, she would not even have enough to pay for a hotel.

As she wandered, she saw an employment agency, but it was shut for the afternoon. However, it reminded her of Templeton's Temps, which Mrs Palmer used frequently. Anna had often seen the address on the envelopes which the prospective servants brought with them. She remembered it was somewhere near Shaftesbury Avenue, as Mrs. Palmer had mentioned going to the theatre there once, so she asked someone the way. If Templeton's turned out to be closed for the afternoon, she did not know what she would do, but she would cross that bridge when she came to it.

She eventually found it in a side street near to Shaftesbury Avenue. As Anna walked up the steps, a girl came hurtling down them, bumping into her. 'I am so sorry,' said the girl in a thick Polish accent. She was of medium height, with wavy auburn hair and bright green eyes.

'Florentyna?' said Anna. Florentyna had once been one of the staff at Silverton, having been sent there as a prisoner of war to work on the farmland. Due to them being short-staffed in the house, Florentyna had soon been moved there. There was very little age difference between the girls, so they had struck up an easy friendship. Anna had even persuaded Florentyna to teach her some Polish, so that if she ever met Janek again, she would be able to speak to him in his own language.

'Miss Anna, how very good to see

you. What are you doing here?'

'I'm looking for a job.'

'Has your . . . has Lady Geraldine thrown you out at last?'

'Yes,' Anna lied, though it was not far from the truth. 'She has.'

'And like everyone else she dismisses, you have no references?'

'Unfortunately, no.'

'Come on inside, and I will help you. Miss Templeton knows of Lady Geraldine's reputation, so you should not have much to worry about.'

'I don't want to bother you,' said Anna.

'It is no bother. I have an appointment in half an hour, but it is just across the road.' Florentyna pointed to a derelict Georgian terrace over the way. Most of the windows were boarded up, and those that were on show were smashed. 'It does not look much now, but it is to be a new hotel called Carmichael's and they want chambermaids. I was going to be early to make a good impression, but it can wait a few minutes. Besides,' said Florentyna, smiling, 'you and Mrs Palmer were the only people who were kind to me at Silverton Hall.'

'Perhaps I could get a job there,' said Anna. 'At Carmichael's, I mean.'

'Yes, we will ask Miss Templeton about it.' Florentyna turned to walk back up the steps.

'Florentyna,' said Anna, catching the girl's arm. 'Can you not introduce me as Anna Silverton? I'm afraid the name would not do me many favours.'

Florentyna thought for a moment, then nodded. 'Yes, you are right. What shall you be called?'

'Anna Palmer.'

'Anna Palmer it is.'

Anna followed Florentyna up the steps to Miss Templeton's agency, not altogether sure whether the lady herself might turn Anna over to the police when she said she had worked at Silverton Hall. Especially if her stepmother had been in touch about new staff, and told her the story of Anna's flight from the police.

Inside there was a small reception area, and at the desk sat a rather formidable-looking woman. Her hair was in a tight bun, and she wore horn-rimmed glasses. As the girls waited, she dealt with an irate client.

'We have asked several times for a Russian speaking au pair,' said the client, who was a young woman of about thirty. She looked like a secretary and spoke with a Russian accent. 'My employer has been most insistent, given that her baby's birth is imminent.'

'I am aware of that, Miss Bazarova, and I have explained to Madame Voronina that Russian-speaking au pairs are very hard to come by. I assure you that as soon as I find someone, I will send her along.'

'It is not good enough,' said Miss Bazarova. 'We will not use this agency again. Never do you have that which we ask for.' She looked like a young woman under a lot of pressure.

'I can only apologise . . . ' the woman

at the desk started to say.

'Yes, yes, you always apologise, Miss Templeton, but never do you do as we ask.'

'I can speak Russian,' said Anna in that language, ignoring Florentyna's warning hand on her arm.

Miss Bazarova turned and looked at Anna with interest. 'You are Russian-born, I can tell,' she said. 'Not from your speech, but from your look.'

'My mother was Russian,' said Anna, still speaking the language. 'I am a little rusty, because it is so long since I was able to speak it.'

'I must concede, you are doing well,' said Miss Bazarova.

'Exactly what is going on here?' asked Miss Templeton in crisp tones.

'This young lady is willing to come to work for us,' said Miss Bazarova.

'That's impossible,' said Miss Templeton. 'I have no idea who this girl is, or what her qualifications are.'

'She was an au pair at Silverton Hall,' said Florentyna, quickly picking up on the tone of the discussion. 'She took care of young Teddy Silverton.' It was not really a lie. Much of Teddy's early care had indeed been left to Anna. 'Only Lady Silverton has done her usual trick of dismissing the poor girl without references.'

'I am still not sure,' said Miss Templeton. 'I know Lady Silverton can be difficult, but . . . '

'We will, of course, pay you the usual commission,' said Miss Bazarova, clearly impressed by the mention of Lady Silverton.

'We do not know why she was dismissed,' said Miss Templeton. Despite that, Anna sensed a shift in her attitude. Her eyes lit up at the mention of a commission.

'You do know Lady Silverton,' said Florentyna. 'It takes very little to displease her. But I can vouch for Anna . . . Palmer's character. I worked at Silverton Hall in the war, and I saw her treat the child with nothing but kindness and patience.' Again that was something which was very true.

'Very well,' said Miss Templeton. 'You're an honest girl, Florentyna, so I know you would not lie to me. There is the question of the paperwork, and putting the girl on file.'

'Yes, yes, we will do that some other time,' said Miss Bazarova. 'For now I need to take this girl to Madam Voronina so she can stop worrying. The doctor is already concerned about her blood pressure. Oh do not look so worried, Miss Templeton. Your commission will be sent immediately. I will take care of it myself.'

Realising that she had no arguments left, Miss Templeton nodded. Anna, Florentyna and Miss Bazarova left the agency together. 'We will get a taxi back to the embassy,' said Miss Bazarova.

'The Russian embassy?' asked Anna.

'Yes, Madame Voronina is the wife of a diplomat.'

'Does that mean we will be going to Russia?'

'Not if my employer can help it,' said

73

Miss Bazarova, tight-lipped.

'Florentyna,' said Anna, turning to her friend. 'Thank you so much for your help.'

'You're very welcome, Anna. As you English say, you fell on your two feet there.'

'Yes, I did rather,' said Anna with a smile.

'Do you have clothes or belongings?' asked Miss Bazarova, frowning, as if she had only just realised that Anna carried nothing with her.

'No. There was no time,' Anna said vaguely, hoping that Miss Bazarova would not press her for details.

'Never mind, we can find you something. You're about my size. Come, we must go.'

Florentyna crossed the road, waving, as the door to the future Carmichael's hotel opened.

★ ★ ★

Janek had opened the door to be free of some of the dust. He saw the young girl crossing the street, and looked beyond her to see two young women standing on the opposite side of the road, watching her. He was about to go back inside when he realised exactly who one of the young women was. She had grown since he last saw her, but it was unmistakably Anna.

'Anna?' he said, going out into the street.

The girl faltered slightly, then said, 'Janek? Is that really you?'

They met in the middle of the street, two strangers who had once been friends through adversity.

The young woman standing on the other side of the road tapped her feet, as if she were in too much of a hurry to witness friends reuniting.

'It really is me,' said Janek. 'How strange. I was only just thinking about you and wondering how you were getting on.'

'She's getting on very well,' said the other, older woman. 'Or she will be if she hurries.'

'I've just got a job as an au pair to a Russian diplomat,' said Anna.

'Well, that's wonderful,' said Janek. 'I'm glad to see you're doing so well.'

'Yes . . . yes, I am. And you? Are you well?'

'I'm busy trying to clean this place up ready for opening, which is why I'm so dusty, but yes, I'm very well.' He could not help noticing what a pretty young woman Anna had become. He would have liked the chance to talk to her more, but her companion was once again tapping her feet. 'Well, don't let me keep you.'

'It was good to see you, Janek,' Anna said awkwardly, following the other woman towards the corner of the road. 'I'm glad you're well.'

'Excuse me,' said the young woman who had been crossing the road when Janek first saw Anna. 'My name is Florentyna. I've come about the chambermaid's post. Can I speak to the boss?'

Janek barely heard her. He was too

busy watching as Anna got into a taxi. 'What? Oh yes. You're already speaking to the boss. Come on in.'

At least he knew Anna was well. It helped to salve his conscience a little. He could get on with what he wanted to do now, without worrying about her anymore. And if he noticed that she looked very pale and frightened, just as she had appeared when he first met her, then he put it down to the nervousness of starting her new post. The woman with her had looked very frightening indeed.

'Come on, Florentyna,' he repeated. 'Can you start straight away?'

'You hardly know me, sir. Don't you want to interview me?'

'You're a friend of Anna's, aren't you? I saw her waving to you.'

'Yes, sir. I've known her since nineteen forty-two. I worked with her at Silverton Hall for a long time.'

'Then I trust you're the right person for the job.'

8

Anna's heart hammered as she sat in the taxi next to Miss Bazarova. Of all the times to bump into Janek! She wished she could have spoken to him a little longer, so she could find out more about his life now. She'd told the truth when she said he looked well. He looked very well indeed. Gone was the scrawny, half-starved teenager of eight years before, to be replaced by a tall, dark and devastatingly handsome young man.

But, she thought, as the taxi travelled through the streets of London, perhaps it was just as well. She could no more involve him in her life now as she could Mrs Palmer. He had helped her once, and she did not want to make him feel responsible for her again. Besides, for all she knew, he would turn her straight over to the police if he found out the truth. He owed her nothing and would probably be horrified to learn she had been accused of trying to harm Teddy.

'I'm sorry we did not have time to talk to your handsome friend for longer,' said Miss Bazarova, pulling Anna out of her reverie. 'We are in such a rush.'

'Is Madame Voronina very difficult?' Anna asked shyly. She doubted anyone could be harder to please than her step-mother, but she had little experience of other grand ladies.

'No, not really. Or I should say, not usually. I don't like to gossip, but it's probably as well to make you aware of the situation into which you are going. The baby Madame Voronina is carrying is her first, and she and her husband have been waiting for it a very long time. She is thirty-eight years old, so the doctors are very concerned about her and the baby. They say she may need bed rest for a long time after the child is born, hence me trying so hard to find an au pair. Mr Voronin is adamant the au pair speaks Russian. Madame is not so concerned about that, but she will do anything she can to make him happy. Unfortunately, trying to make him happy is causing her more stress. But she is a dear woman, so do not be afraid. Before I take you to meet her, you can freshen up and I will loan you some of my clothes.'

'Thank you, Miss Bazarova.'

'Since we are to be working together, call me Tasha. And I hope I may call you Anna.'

'Yes, of course. Thank you, Tasha.' Anna looked at the other girl under her eyelashes. She had thought her fierce, but now she realised Tasha was only fiercely loyal to Madame Voronina. 'You say that Madame has no wish to return to Russia.'

'No.' Tasha looked around, as if afraid of being overheard. 'Please do not repeat this, otherwise Madame will be in great trouble, but Madame likes the freedom of the West. In Russia it is not so free. Even now I am afraid that I have said too much to you.'

'I shan't betray your trust, Tasha; don't worry. I lived in Russia as a child, so I know what it's like there. We were lucky, because my mother could travel all over the world as a ballerina, so we did not have to live there much.'

'Your mother was a ballerina? What was her name? I love the ballet. Perhaps I saw her.' Just as Anna was afraid she might have to answer that question, the taxi stopped outside a grand house in a leafy square in the north of London. 'Ah, we're here,' said Tasha. 'We'll save this conversation until later. I'm sure we'll have much to talk about, both being from the Motherland. It is strange, is it not, how one can love their country yet hate living there?' Tasha paid the taxi driver and led Anna into the house and up a flight of stairs.

Half an hour later, Anna was dressed in a dark blue skirt suit with a white blouse. She could not remember ever dressing so elegantly, at least not as a young woman. The last time she had dressed up was when her mother was alive. Not wanting to get lost in sad memories, Anna quickly followed Tasha back downstairs and into a grand drawing room.

It had been furnished in an ornate Russian style, and as such, delighted Anna. A large gold samovar stood on a sideboard. It had been a long time since she had drunk tea from one and once again she was reminded of her mother, and the days when they had taken tea together, revelling in every delicious cup.

Sitting at the far end of the drawing room, at a writing desk, sat the most beautiful woman Anna had ever seen. She had jet-black hair, pulled back tightly from her head, and alabaster skin. Even though she was with child, she looked very slender, with only the bump on her tummy giving a clue as to her condition. Anna had the strange feeling they had met before. 'You are back, Tasha,' she said, with a smile.

'And I see you have brought me a new friend.'

'This is Anna Palmer, Madame,' Tasha said in Russian. 'I have engaged her as your au pair. She speaks Russian.'

'Come closer, child,' said Madame Voronina, also speaking in Russian. 'Let me look at you.'

Hesitating, Anna took a few steps towards Madame, feeling quite intimidated. 'How do you do, Madame. I hope you will be pleased with my work.'

'Anna? Anna Palmer, you say,' said Madame.

'Yes, that is correct.'

'I knew a little girl called Anna once. You could very easily be her. Or her mother. In fact you could not be anyone else. It is Anna, is it not? Natalia's daughter?'

At that, tears pricked Anna's eyes. Partly because Madame knew her mother and partly because she feared being sent away. 'Yes, that is correct.'

'And you're working as an au pair?'

'Yes, Madame. I don't mind, really.'

Madame turned to Tasha to explain. 'Anna's mother and I were in the ballet together, a long time ago.' Madame held out her hands to Anna. 'Please, don't look so fearful, child. Natalia Andreyev's daughter is a friend to me. You must tell me everything that has happened to you.'

'I . . . ' Anna licked her lips, hardly knowing where to start, or even how much she could trust Madame with.

'Oh but I am selfish. You must be hungry and thirsty. You look exhausted. Tasha, take Anna to the kitchen and find her something to eat and drink. We will resume our talk tomorrow. The doctor insists I go to bed early every night, so I will see you in the morning, Anna. Oh, I am so happy to see you. I've thought of you and Natalia so often over the years.'

Dazed and a little confused, Anna followed Tasha to the kitchen. What a day it had been. First bumping into Florentyna just when she needed help, then overhearing Tasha's conversation with Miss Templeton, before seeing Janek, and now meeting an old friend of her mother's. If anyone had told her that such coincidences happened, she would have scoffed at them. She found herself looking upwards, even though all she could see were the ornate covings on the ceiling rather than the heavens.

Eight years earlier when she had been frightened and alone, she had met Janek on the train and he had put aside his own problems to help her. After that, Mrs Palmer had taken care of her. Today, when she was also frightened and alone, more help had come. Despite her father's indifference and her step-mother's unkind behaviour, Anna could not say she had ever really been uncared for, even if her life had not always been a happy one.

She smiled, but it was tinged with sadness. She could not help being convinced that her mother had always watched over her and kept her safe from harm.

9

One of the first things Anna did when she received her first month's wages was to return Mr Stephens's ten shillings to him with a note apologising. She walked across London, pushing the baby Nikolai Voronin in his pram so that she did not give away her actual whereabouts. Tasha accompanied her for the walk, though Anna kept the true nature of it from her.

Nikolai had been born perfectly well, but Madame Voronina had been ordered to take complete bed rest. She saw Nikolai in the mornings and evenings, but the rest of the time it was left to Anna to care for him. Not that she minded. He was a very placid, happy child. She began to see how a baby might prosper with a mother and father who loved him dearly.

Mr Voronin had frightened Anna at

first. A large man with a loud, jocular voice, he put her in mind of pictures she had seen of Tsar Nicholas. Mr Voronin was apt to be a little sharper with the staff than his wife if they did things wrong, but Anna sensed immediately that there was no bad in him, mainly because he always came afterwards to apologise. She also sensed he was under a lot of pressure as a diplomat from the Russian government.

'We were not popular in this country or America,' he said over dinner one night. 'And . . . ' he looked over his shoulder, even though no one else was in the room, 'given the policies of the Soviet Union since the war, I cannot always blame them.'

Despite her status as an au pair, both Mr Voronin and Madame Voronina had practically turned Anna into one of the family, insisting she eat with them and Tasha. As if guessing that she had very little of her own, Madame had also insisted on buying her new clothes, despite Anna's protests.

'You are not to refuse,' Madame had said, just before young Nikolai was born. 'It is the least I can do to help you, after all the time you have been alone. I should have done more when you were a child, after poor Natalia died. Besides, it does not look good if we allow our au pair to have holes in her shoes whilst we dress well.'

Anna did not remember telling Madame she had been alone in the world, and she did not really consider she had, what with Mrs Palmer to take care of her. But it was true that when it came to family, Anna had no one. So Madame had bought her several new outfits and a warm winter coat.

As they walked across London, Tasha was unusually quiet. Not that Anna minded. She had her own thoughts. She had put a message for Mrs Palmer in the note, telling her she was sorry she had failed her. She hoped that the good lady would think of her kindly. Nevertheless, feeling it was rude not to engage in conversation, Anna asked,

'Are you alright, Tasha? You seem preoccupied.'

'It is all this talk of returning home,' said Tasha. She spoke in a low voice, acutely aware that a security officer walked just a few feet behind them. His name was Sergei and he had only recently been assigned to them, for reasons that worried everyone. 'It makes Madame unhappy. She does not want Nikolai raised in Russia, and even though Mr Voronin tries not to say so publicly . . . ' Tasha looked around furtively, much in the same way Mr Voronin had done at dinner, 'he does not wish to return either. They have been happy in London, and so have I.'

'Is it really so bad in Russia?' whispered Anna. Because her mother had been a ballerina, and allowed to travel, she had not really seen much of her homeland.

'It is worse than bad. People have to queue for food, even when there is no war. Families have to live together in tiny apartments. There is a waiting list to buy a car. Those in government live well, yet the rest of us have to endure austere lives.'

'So Mr Voronin should be all right, surely. He is in government.'

'He is a diplomat yes, but . . . ' Tasha looked around again, smiling at Sergei. He did not smile back. He never did. 'He is not always as discreet as he should be when he criticises the government, so he has been warned he may be recalled at any moment. No wonder Madame is unwell. It is not her body, but her nerves which ail her. Mr Voronin has become too comfortable here, I think, so he forgets that he has to be careful what he says. Even now I am afraid to talk to you.'

'I would never betray you, Tasha.' The girls had become firm friends in the short time that Anna had been working for the Voronins. They were united in their wish to make Madame's life as easy as possible. It was not that Madame was demanding. It was quite the opposite. Because she had a kind heart and only saw kindness wherever she looked, they were protective of her. So they shielded her from the frightening security officers, and the other officials who seemed to want to interfere with every aspect of the Voronins' life.

'I know you wouldn't, Anna. But I must warn you that if there are ever any problems, you get out of the embassy as soon as possible. You have British citizenship because of your father, so you do not have to go back to Russia.'

Since they had made friends, and because Madame knew the details anyway, Anna had trusted Tasha with some of the truth about her father and her time at Silverton Hall. She had told neither of them about Teddy's fall, fearing they would not trust her with Nikolai if they knew. They both assumed she had left there because she was unhappy and she did not disabuse them of that notion. It was not entirely untrue. In the first few days she lived with the Voronins, she would lie awake at night, wondering if an omission were as big a sin as a lie. She hoped not.

'So,' said Tasha, putting her arm in Anna's as they strode along on a crisp autumn afternoon, 'tell me more about the handsome Janek.'

'I barely know him,' said Anna. 'I mean . . . we did know each other well when we were children. We travelled through France together, to escape the war. He took care of me. I was a burden to him, I know that now. But at the time he was my only friend.'

'I wonder what he was doing at that hotel.'

'It looked like he was working there. His father owned a hotel in Poland, so perhaps he has managed to get a job as a doorman or something.'

'Yes, that's probably it. We should go there when it's open. If we can get the security men to agree to it.'

'No!'

'Why?' asked Tasha. 'The way you looked at him, and the way he looked right back at you outside Miss Templeton's it seemed to me you liked each other very much.'

'He's like a brother to me,' said Anna. 'When I lived at Silverton Hall, I used to dream that he would return for me and we would live as brother and sister. Like a proper family.' Those dreams seemed silly now that she had grown up. She recognised them for what they were: a child's fantasy to get her through the unhappy days.

'Such a man should not be a girl's brother!' Tasha protested. 'Oh well. If you do not want him, I shall have him.'

Anna tried to laugh, except part of her still thought of Janek as her very own, because of what they had been through together. Yet Tasha was pretty and a nice person, when she was not taking on anyone who upset Madame. If Janek liked her, she would be happy for them. At least that was what she told herself, so that she could convince herself that she was not in any way jealous of her friend's interest in him.

10

Six Years Later

Sixteen-year-old Teddy Silverton decided to seek refuge in his father's study. Anna would not have recognised the chubby boy in the tall and handsome young man he had become.

Unfortunately, Teddy quickly found out he would not have the room to himself. His mother was in there, frantically rooting through paperwork. 'What are you looking for, Mother?' he asked when she looked up, startled. His father would have been most upset to see the state she had made of his desk. Always orderly, Sir Lionel did not like anyone moving his paperwork.

'Oh it's you, Teddy. Do you have the combination to your father's safe?'

'No, of course not.'

'Really? I thought Father might have

given it to you so you can run the estate. Oh I forgot. He doesn't trust you, does he? Never mind.' Geraldine sighed. 'Can you get it for me, darling?'

'Mother, he's convalescing. I don't think we should be bothering him. What do you need? If it's money, I have some of my allowance left.'

'You are a dear sweet boy, but you really don't understand how urgent things have become,' said Geraldine. Her voice held a brittle note. Even though her love for him could be cloying at times, it did not always stop Teddy from feeling the sharp end of her tongue when she was distressed.

'In what way?'

'In the way of you losing your inheritance. I need to see your father's will, so I can be sure. You must understand that, dearest boy.'

'Mother, I'm not worried about my inheritance, so I don't think you should be. And you'll have an annuity, whether or not. So you won't be short of money either.'

'No wonder your father is so frustrated with you. I know what you're thinking,' Geraldine began to whine. 'You'll go off to this medical school when you're eighteen, and you won't care about me anymore.' She wiped her eyes on her handkerchief, sniffing loudly. 'And after all I've done to ensure you take over Silverton Hall. And it will be yours, no matter what. Unless you intend to turn it into a hospital.'

'That's not a bad idea,' said Teddy.

'I was joking!'

'Even so, it isn't a bad idea. With the new National Health Service, they're going to need more hospitals.'

'I can imagine. All those poor people bothering doctors with their pathetic ailments. I really don't know why you want to waste your time.'

'It's called humanity, Mother. And perhaps a way of putting right a wrong.'

'Oh, don't start all that again.'

'I told you that I'd lied about Anna. And it's been on my conscience every day since.' Teddy had sleepless nights over how badly he had treated his half-sister. His biggest wish was to tell her he was sorry, but he had no idea where she was. All they knew was that she was living somewhere in London, because Stephens had received a letter from her with a ten-shilling note to repay her debt. Mrs Palmer had sobbed over that note, and mentioned it every day until she retired and went to the seaside, with Mr Stephens following not long after. Now the household was run by staff that came and went in very quick order, unable to put up with his mother's tantrums and rudeness.

'I'm not so sure you did lie, Teddy. After all, why else would she run away if she were not guilty?'

'Because you frightened her. Because she thought she was going to be arrested and sent to jail.'

'She should have been! In fact if I have my way, she still will be.' Geraldine took a deep breath. 'Get me the combination to your father's safe,

Teddy. If you don't do it, I shan't let you go to France with Freddie Fortescue's family this summer.'

'Mother!'

'I mean it. You're not eighteen yet, young man, so you still need our permission to go.'

Geraldine stormed from the room, clearly convinced that Teddy would do as she asked.

He slumped into his father's chair and began pondering. What was his mother really looking for? He had little doubt that she would know the entire contents of Sir Lionel's will. It was the sort of thing she made it her business to know. Being a rather placid, easily handled man, it would have taken Geraldine very little time to get the truth from Sir Lionel. Unless she suspected that he withheld some information from her. Even if he had, what could she do about it? Unless she planned to bully Teddy's father into taking out the offending clause.

If there was such a clause, Teddy

believed it had something to do with Anna. Sighing to himself, he also started sifting through the papers on his father's desk, but tidied them up as he did so, putting them into orderly piles. Since rationing ended, the bills were piling up, due to there being no more checks on his mother's spending.

Teddy supposed he ought to take care of the bills, to ensure that they were paid, so that the tradesmen did not withdraw their wares. He also understood better than his mother how small businesses could fail when rich people did not settle their accounts.

Smiling to himself as he totted up the accounts, he remembered how he had told Anna he hated arithmetic. It was only when he learned that doctors needed to be good at sums that he began to apply himself, until even his teacher commented on his improvement. He hoped his half-sister would be proud of him, but feared that she may actually hate him for the lie he had told. With good reason, too.

A couple of hours later, with all the paperwork completed, Teddy put things away in the top drawer. The drawer stuck a bit as he pushed it in, so he had to put his hand under to give it a shove. That was when he felt the slip of card, taped to the underside of the desk. Taking the drawer out and turning it over, Teddy found what his mother had searched for so frantically. The combination to his father's safe.

It occurred to Teddy that he could take a look, and perhaps find out what his mother wanted, without bothering his father. Just at that moment the front door slammed shut. He looked at the clock, which said two o'clock.

'Izzy,' he said with a smile, quickly putting the drawer and its contents back in place, before bounding into the hall.

Bounding out into the hall, looking more like the child Anna knew than the young man, Teddy grinned at their visitor. 'Good afternoon, Izzy,' he said.

'Good afternoon, Master Teddy,' Izzy

said in her gentle Scottish tones. She was nineteen years old, and quite the prettiest girl Teddy had ever seen. Her hair hung in soft auburn waves, and her face, devoid of make up, was covered in freckles.

'I've told you not to call me that. It's just Teddy, right?'

'Your mother says I must call you Master Teddy.' Izzy lowered her voice. 'To be honest I'm more afraid of her than you.' That was what Teddy liked best about Izzy. She was not afraid to say what she thought. Despite saying she was afraid of his mother, Izzy had often been known to put Lady Geraldine in her place. Even his mother was in awe of the medical profession — despite not wanting her son joining them — so she seldom argued back. 'How is Sir Lionel today?'

'He's very well, and looking forward to your visit.'

'I doubt he'll say that when I start exercising those legs of his,' Izzy laughed.

'Can I help you? It will be good practice for when I become a doctor,' said Teddy. Since his father had suffered a minor stroke, Teddy had taken a great interest in his recovery, though whether that was down to helping his father, or the fact that it was when Izzy first turned up in their lives, he could not honestly say. He loved his father, and did not wish him harm, but their relationship had always been rather distant.

'Very well. Just don't get in the way.' Izzy started up the stairs, then paused when she heard Teddy hurrying up after her. 'Teddy, you're a sweet boy and please don't take this the wrong way. It's just something I've been thinking of saying for a while. Please don't think that there can ever be anything between us.' He loved her even more for her directness. 'There can't be. You're too young for me for a start. Then there's the fact you're in a different social class, and I doubt your parents would approve. But you are a sweetie.'

'I'm not that sweet,' said Teddy. 'Really I'm not. If you knew of the horrible thing I'd done . . . '

'You'll have to tell me all about it one day, but to be honest I can't imagine you're capable of anything horrible.'

11

Anna found it hard to believe that six years had passed since she had started working for the Voronins. Rationing had ended, and there was a pretty young queen on the throne. Britain was finally recovering from the austerity of the war years, and had become more prosperous. This was evident in the cheerful music coming from the cafes and bars, and the bright clothes in the shops.

They had been six happy years for Anna. Madame Voronina had been a mentor to her, teaching her not just things about her own land she had not known, but also how to dress properly and use make-up to good effect.

'Not that you need much,' Madame had said. 'You are a naturally lovely girl, with good colouring, so whatever you do, don't go plastering your lips with bright red.'

Although Madame agreed she could never take the place of Anna's mother, she treated her like a daughter. Madame was just the same with Tasha. Although the girls were employed by the Voronins and therefore paid a salary, it never felt that way.

'You girls are my rock,' Madame would sometimes say. 'You make this family what it is.'

Anna also had a best friend in Tasha. Often Tasha would accompany Anna and young Nikolai to the park, just so they could chat.

That morning was different. Anna was alone with Nikolai in the park, and her young heart was troubled. She did not like to complain, knowing how fortunate she had been to find the Voronins when she needed them most. But over the past few weeks, she had often been left out of conversations, or discussions ended when she left the room. Only that morning, she and Tasha had been due to go to the park with Nikolai, but

Madame had called Tasha back.

'We could go later,' Anna had offered.

'No, no, you go, Anna,' said Madame. 'Take Nicky to Hyde Park. I will give you money for a taxi.'

Hyde Park was quite a long way from the Voronins' house in North London. She seldom went into central London, preferring to stay on the outskirts.

Going to Hyde Park meant that Anna and Nicky would be gone most of the morning. Anna could not help feeling that she was being got out of the way for some reason. And it was not the first time it had happened.

Sighing, and watching Nicky feed the ducks on a bright spring morning, she told herself not to be so childish. Of course she could not expect to be privy to every private conversation between Madame and Tasha. But it was not only that. Several times over the past weeks, she had been told to take dinner with Nicky, and not with the family. She was beginning to fear that she had done something to displease Madame.

'Anna!' Nicky called. He was standing near the base of a tree.

'Don't climb the tree!' Anna cried, panicking.

'I am not going to climb it,' said Nicky. 'I will spoil my new trousers.'

Anna smiled. She had never met a child so fussy about how he looked. Nicky already had the look of a little diplomat.

'It is you, Anna,' said Nicky.

'What?'

'This picture on this tree. It is you.'

Anna walked across and just as Nicky had said, there was a flyer with a picture of her. It was faded, suggesting it had been there for a long time. Anna took it off the tree carefully and put it in her pocket. There was a telephone number on the bottom, and a message asking to contact a Mr and Mrs Stephens. She became afraid that the money she had returned to Mr Stephens had not reached him. Perhaps he was angry with her for taking it and wanted to have her arrested. Her heart beat rapidly.

'Come on, Nicky,' she said, taking the little boy's hand. 'We had better return home.'

'Not yet, Anna. Mama said we're to be sure not to return until lunch time.'

'When did she say that?'

'This morning. She said, 'Make sure you and Anna stay at the park until lunchtime'.'

'I see . . . ' It seemed to Anna that a cloud passed over the sky. Not only was Madame trying to get her out of the way, but she was involving Nicky in their subterfuge. 'Oh well,' said Anna, determined not to let it bother her. 'I think that calls for an ice cream, don't you? Unless you are afraid it will spoil your clothes,' she teased.

'I think I can manage not to make a mess. I am nearly seven.'

'In ten months' time!' Anna laughed. She would not be miserable in front of Nicky. He was not to blame for whatever was happening. He merely obeyed his mama as any good child should.

They wandered through the park to the ice cream van, then sat on a bench, eating a 99 cornet. 'Which do you think is best?' asked Nicky. 'The ice cream or the chocolate flake?'

'Hmm, I like them both.'

'Personally I like the strawberry sauce,' said a voice from a few feet away from them.

'Hello, Anna.'

'Janek . . . ' Anna almost dropped her ice cream. In all her years in London, she had never once bumped into him again. Now here he was, looking even more handsome than the last time she had seen him. Along with anyone else who read the newspapers, Anna had quickly learned that Janek was not an employee at Carmichael's, but one of the owners. In fact, he was very much considered the only owner, with his sleeping partner keeping very much out of the spotlight. The company had also become a chain, opening hotels in New

York and Paris. Carmichael's hotels were synonymous with 'olde worlde' charm, and the sort of elegance that had been lost due to the ravages of war.

'It's very good to see you again, Anna,' he said, giving her a devastating smile.

'How do you do,' said Nicky, standing up and holding out a slightly sticky hand. 'I am Nikolai Voronin.'

'I am very pleased to meet you, Mr Voronin,' said Janek, holding out his own hand. 'Am I to assume that you are Anna's intended?' He grinned.

'No, silly. She is far too old for me. She is our au pair, though Mama says I'm not allowed to say that because Anna is family now.'

'I'm glad to hear it,' said Janek. 'I'm also glad to see you doing so well, Anna. I've often thought of you.'

Anna, rendered speechless by seeing him again, managed a smile. 'Not as well as you're doing, I notice.'

'Carmichael's hotels are doing well, yes. You should come and see us one day. I'll treat you and young Mr Voronin here to a high tea. Would you like that, Mr Voronin?'

'I would love to,' said Nicky. 'And as you're a friend of Anna's you may call me Nicky. I've always longed to stay at Carmichael's.'

Anna laughed. It was news to her. She could only assume that Nicky found Janek as impressive-looking as she did.

'Will you come?' This time Janek spoke only to Anna. 'Please.'

'Yes, we would like that, wouldn't we, Nicky?'

'What about tomorrow?'

'Tomorrow? I er . . . '

'The thing is, I have to fly out to New York the next day and I may be gone for a week or two. I would like to see you again before I go.'

'Yes; if Madame Voronina agrees, we'll come tomorrow,' said Anna.

'Janek!' A woman's voice rang across the park. Anna looked and saw a very glamorous young woman standing a few feet away. 'Janek, where did you get to?'

'I'm sorry, Mary. I've just met an old friend. Mary Carmichael, this is Anna . . . '

'Palmer,' Anna cut in quickly. Whilst Madame knew about her father and Silverton Hall, Nicky did not, and she was reluctant to confuse the child.

'That's just what I was going to say,' said Janek. 'I've spoken to Florentyna quite a few times about you.'

'You have?' Anna looked at him wide-eyed.

'Of course. I'm sorry you had such a bad time at . . . '

Before he could say anymore, Mary had covered the distance between them and put her arm in his. 'Janek, darling, you can talk to your little friend another time. We have to go and meet Mike for lunch, remember?'

'Forgive me, Anna,' said Janek. 'Business and duty call. But I shall see you and Nicky tomorrow.'

Anna watched as they walked away,

whilst Mary picked imaginary bits of fluff from Janek's pristine coat.

'We can go, can't we, Anna?' Nicky sat back down next to her, pulling at her sleeve.

'I'm not sure, Nicky . . . ' It was ridiculous that she should feel so jealous of Mary Carmichael. She and Janek were virtual strangers now. This did not explain why the two very brief times she had seen him since their adventure, her heart flipped uncontrollably. He did not belong to her, just because they had shared a desperate experience a very long time ago. She wished him to be happy, and if Mary made him happy, so be it.

'I shall ask Mama,' said Nicky. 'I'm sure she will allow it.'

12

'She's a pretty girl,' said Izzy. 'Is she your sweetheart?'

Teddy looked up, startled. He had not heard Izzy come into the kitchen. He shook his head. 'No, this is Anna, my half-sister.'

'I had no idea you had a sister,' said Izzy.

'I've just made a cup of tea. Would you like some?' asked Teddy.

'Your mother would have a fit if she knew you were in the kitchen. But yes I would like one very much, thank you.' Izzy sat down at the kitchen table.

'You can have half of my luncheon meat sandwich if you want. I haven't touched it yet. It's all very well Mother saying I can't come into the kitchen, but since she frightens away most of the staff, I don't have much choice. Anyway, times are changing, Izzy. The days of spoilt little rich boys living off their trust fund and unable to fend for themselves have gone. I just wish Mother would understand that.'

'You're going to be quite a man when you grow up, Teddy, do you know that?'

He put a cup of tea in front of Izzy and smiled. 'I think I'm quite grown up enough.'

Izzy laughed indulgently. 'Oh, in a couple more years maybe. So, tell me about Anna.'

Teddy sat back down in his own seat, and once again offered half his sandwich to Izzy, which she took gratefully. 'Do you remember me telling you the other day that I'd done something awful?'

'Yes. And I said I doubted it.'

'Well, I did. Because of me, Anna was accused of attempting to . . . well to cause me serious harm. Then she ran away and I don't know where she is. I just wish I could find her, and tell her I'm sorry.' Once he had started to speak, Teddy could not stop himself. He wanted Izzy to know everything.

'Slow down, Teddy,' she said, putting her hand over his. He wished he could hold her hand forever, but she had made it clear she thought him too young for her. 'And tell me everything from the beginning.'

So that was what Teddy did. He told Izzy all about how Anna had come into their lives, right up to what had happened when he climbed the tree. By the time he finished, he took a deep, cleansing breath.

'Oh, Teddy, you were only a little boy,' said Izzy. 'You're being much too hard on yourself. If Anna running away was anyone's fault, then I'm sorry to say it was your mother's. She must have known Anna would not really do such a thing.'

'She wouldn't do anything like that,' said Teddy vehemently. 'I used to tell her she was a peach of a girl and she really was. Only Anna and Mrs Palmer spoke to me when I was at home. I mean really spoke to me, like I was somebody.'

'You are somebody.'

'You wouldn't think it, from the way Mother and Father speak to me. Oh, the old man's not so bad really. He's just as frightened of Mother as everyone else is. But mother only ever spoke to me to scold or to mollycoddle me.'

'She loves you very much, Teddy. You can't criticise her for that.' If Izzy was anything, she was fair-minded, and always tried to see the best in people. 'Maybe it was genuine fear when you fell out of the tree that caused her to accuse Anna of causing it.'

Teddy shook his head. 'No, she hardly bothered about my injuries. Such as they were. I had a bit of a bruise on my head and my leg, that's all. My pride took the biggest beating.'

'Has no one heard from Anna since?'

'She wrote a letter to Stephens, our old butler, and sent him a ten-shilling note. That was about a month later. We didn't know it at the time, but she'd borrowed the money off him. All she said was that she hoped I was all right and that Mrs Palmer would understand why she had to run away. It was posted in London, so Mrs Palmer and Mr Stephens had some thoughts of looking for her there. I don't know if they ever found her. Soon after, they both left. Mrs Palmer was going to run a guesthouse in Filey with her sister, and Mr Stephens was going to lodge with them.'

'Perhaps we could go and ask her,' suggested Izzy.

'Who, Mrs Palmer?'

'Why not? It's possible they found Anna but just didn't tell you.'

'Because they were angry with me, you mean?'

'No, I was thinking more to protect her from your mother. I really think we could go in search of Mrs Palmer.'

'We?'

'I've got a few days off and I fancy a trip to the seaside.'

'I'm surprised you want to spend any time with me after what I've told you.'

'And I've told you to stop upsetting yourself over something that happened when you were a little boy. I'm sure Anna doesn't blame you.'

'What if she does blame me, Izzy? What if I find her and she hates me?'

'From what you've said of her, Teddy, she doesn't seem like that sort of girl.'

'It depends what's happened to her in the meantime, doesn't it? Who knows what she's suffered?'

'Now you're being melodramatic! You told me yourself that Anna somehow managed to escape from war-torn Europe when she was only ten years old. It seems to me that if she's resourceful enough to do that, she's resourceful enough to survive anything.'

'I hope you're right, Izzy. I really do.'

'So, when shall we go to the seaside?'

13

'I think a high tea at Carmichael's is a wonderful idea,' said Madame. She was sitting in her bedroom, applying make-up. 'I would like to meet Mr Dabrowski myself. I had no idea he was the one who escaped from Europe with you, Anna.'

'I knew,' said Tasha, who was sitting on the bed. 'I kept trying to persuade Anna to go and visit him, but she put it off every time.'

'I didn't want to impose on what was only a very brief acquaintance,' said Anna. In reality she had been afraid that Janek would believe she only wanted his friendship now that he was rich. The more famous he became, the more difficult it was for her to go and see him. It was as if a wall a thousand feet high had been built between them. 'But now I have been invited, Madame, I am sure he would not mind you accompanying us this afternoon. You too, Tasha. I would ring up and ask first, of course, so as not to be rude.' Anna wondered if Madame were offended at being left out of the invitation.

A look passed between Madame and Tasha — one of their increasingly secretive looks that gave Anna the impression they were carrying on a private conversation about things to which she was not privy. 'No, no,' said Madame. 'I have things to do, and I need Tasha's help. You and Nicky must go and tell us all about Carmichael's. I hear the high tea is the very best in London.'

Anna and Nicky arrived at Carmichael's at around four o'clock that afternoon. Even in her best yellow summer dress and pristine white gloves, she felt out of place. As the papers had said, Carmichael's harked back to a bygone age of quiet elegance. The interior of the hotel was decorated in the art deco style, lit with Tiffany lamps, and with a few nods towards classical architecture, it really was the most beautiful building.

She was acutely aware of her heels clicking on the white marble floor as they entered and wished she could walk more quietly. Her voice was barely above a whisper when she informed the desk clerk of her name. 'Mr Dabrowski is expecting us, I believe,' said Anna. 'Of course if he is busy . . . ' If he were busy, she could go away and stop her heart from fluttering so rapidly.

'I am not busy, Anna,' said a voice from behind her. 'I have been waiting for you. Hello, young Nicky. How are you today?'

'I'm very well thank you, Mr Dabrowski. We came by tube! Mama doesn't usually let us, but she said we could today. It was very exciting. I'm very happy to be here.'

'I'm glad to hear it. Whereas Anna looks as if she would like to run away.'

'I feel scruffy in such sumptuous

surroundings,' said Anna, trying to make light of her nerves.

'You look lovely, like the epitome of summer,' said Janek.

Oh dear, thought Anna, now he would think she was fishing for compliments. 'Thank you,' was all she could manage to say.

'I thought we'd take tea up on my terrace,' said Janek. 'It has a wonderful view of the city.'

'Brilliant!' said Nicky.

That calmed Anna a little. At least if they were in private, she would not be so aware of how she compared with the truly elegant ladies who sat in the foyer, drinking tea and chatting eagerly about their Harrods purchases.

High tea at Carmichael's was everything it was said to be. As Anna and Nicky looked out over London, with Janek pointing out landmarks to them, a member of staff brought up plates full of tiny sandwiches and small cakes. At pride of place in the middle of the table was an enormous fruit cake.

'Can we take some back for Mama and Papa?' Nicky asked.

'Nicky,' Anna chided gently.

'Of course you may,' Janek interrupted. 'I should have thought to include them in the invitation. I hope you'll forgive me, Nicky, but I was so eager to be able to see Anna again, I completely forgot my manners.'

The afternoon seemed to be made up of Janek addressing comments to or about Anna through Nicky, so she followed his lead. Having Nicky there almost as a chaperone helped to ease some of the tension.

'Are you very rich?' Nicky asked Janek as they ate their sandwiches. Anna was about to chide him again but thankfully Janek laughed.

'I don't do too badly. It was not always so, as Anna will tell you. When we first met, I was a starving teenager.'

'Yes, I remember,' Anna said. 'Janek ate all my bread and cheese. Not that I minded. He needed it more than I did.'

'Mama says that people in Russia are

very hungry,' said Nicky. 'And that Russia now owns Poland. Is that true, Mr Dabrowski?'

'No, Russia is merely borrowing Poland at the moment. They will never truly own my country. We belong to ourselves.'

'Have you been able to return?' asked Anna.

Janek shook his head. 'No. Sadly, if I were to go there, I might not be allowed to leave again. I am applying for British citizenship. Perhaps then I will have a chance to return. And you, will you go back to Russia when the Voronins do?'

'I don't really know,' said Anna.

Bored with the grown-up conversation, Nicky took a sandwich and went to look out over London.

'They always talk of being called back,' said Anna in a quiet voice. 'I've worked with the Voronins for just over six years, and every day they have the same fear. But I've come to believe it's a little like a child worrying about a monster under the bed. Or at least I did.'

'Something has changed?' asked Janek.

'I don't know . . . it's just that lately . . . ' Anna paused and checked where Nicky was. He could come to no harm on the terrace as the railings were too high, but she did not want him to think she was criticising his parents. 'I've felt that something is going on,' she continued. 'They're always eager to get me out of the way and I can't help wondering if I've displeased them. Yet Madame is as kind as she's always been. Oh I'm sorry, I shouldn't be bothering you with my worries.'

'We're friends, Anna, and have been for a long time. You can always come to me with your worries. You never told me why you left Silverton Hall. Florentyna told me they were very unkind to you there.'

Anna shook her head. 'No, not really. I mean, my father barely noticed me and my step-mother hated me, but no more than she hates most people. Mrs Palmer — do you remember her? — and Mr Stephens the butler were always kind enough. They made it bearable.'

'Yes, I remember Mrs Palmer. A frighteningly efficient woman but a good ally to have, I should think. So why did you leave?'

Anna wanted to tell Janek the truth, hoping that he would understand, but the secret of what happened with Teddy was something she had locked up inside herself for so long, she could not put it into words. What if Janek decided he did not want to be her friend anymore? What if he told the Voronins and they fired her, because they no longer trusted her with Nicky? 'I just decided I wanted a different life for myself. Admittedly I'm still a servant, but it's no hardship when it's for such a wonderful family.'

'I'm glad the Voronins treat you well, but I still don't think you should be a servant. Not with your background.'

'My background is that of an

illegitimate child, Janek. My beginnings were hardly respectable.'

'Such things should not matter in a civilised society.'

'Oh but it is a so-called civilised society which frowns upon such things. You should know better than anyone what it is to be an outsider. I presume there is a reason the hotel is called Carmichael's and not Dabrowski's.'

'You are right. I was afraid that with all the anti-European feeling after the war, naming the hotel Dabrowski's would not guarantee its success.'

'So we are both victims of either real or imagined prejudices.'

'Perhaps that's why we made friends in the first place, Anna. We recognised a kindred spirit.' He smiled, and it seemed to Anna as if the sun shone a little brighter. 'And now, because I owe it you, I am going to let you have the last cheese sandwich.' He pushed the plate towards her.

'I would not deprive you of it,' she said, laughing. 'Besides, I owe you much more. You came back for me when the train crashed. I think at the very least that has earned you the last cheese sandwich.'

Janek became more serious. 'I didn't come back to you when I promised I would. After I left you with the Silvertons. And for that I am sorry.'

'I was hurt at first,' Anna admitted. 'But as I've grown older I realised that it would never have been possible. I was not your responsibility for a start. I understand that you said what you had to say to calm me when I was afraid, and I bless you for that.' She did not tell Janek of the nights she had sat by her window, waiting for him to come back. Only as the war went on and she grew older had she finally admitted the truth to herself: that he was not coming back and probably never meant to.

'Thank you. I promise you that I will never turn my back on you again, Anna. I am your friend and if you ever need me, you only have to ask.'

'But I am still not your responsibility.'

'What if I decide that you are?'

They looked across the table at each other for what seemed like an eternity, but which could only have been a few seconds.

Nicky came bounding back to the table and picked up the last cheese sandwich, biting into it with a huge smile on his face.

'Well,' said Janek, laughing. 'That settles the argument of who gets the last cheese sandwich.'

14

Once Anna had relaxed a little more in Janek's company, the afternoon seemed to pass all too quickly. She wished she could spend more time with him, but it was getting late and she needed to get Nicky back home.

'Thank you so much for inviting us,' said Anna when Janek took them back downstairs to the foyer.

'Yes, thank you,' said Nicky. 'May we come again?'

'You certainly may, my young friend,' said Janek. 'But only if you always promise to bring Anna with you.'

'Oh yes, we go everywhere together,' said Nicky.

'And you must tell your mama and papa that they are also welcome,' Janek said.

'And Tasha?' said Nicky,

'Mr Dabrowski can't feed all of

London,' Anna laughed.

'Not all of London,' Janek replied. 'Just the very special people.'

'And who might they be?' asked Anna. She had hoped to bring the conversation around to Mary Carmichael, but had shied away from it, afraid of what she might learn.

'Anyone who is a friend to you, of course,' said Janek.

At that moment a man came from the kitchens, carrying a big parcel. 'The cake, Mr Dabrowski,' he said, handing the parcel to Janek.

'Here you go, Nicky,' said Janek. 'It may be a bit heavy for you to carry, so I'll give it to Anna. It is a whole fruit cake for your mama and papa and Tasha.'

'Oh really,' said Anna, 'it's too generous. I'm sure Nicky only meant to ask for a slice each, is that not right, Nicky?' Nicky nodded, his eyes wide open at the size of the cake which Janek gave to Anna.

'It is not too much. It is very little,'

said Janek. 'But I'm only giving it to you if you promise to come again.'

'Oh we will,' said Nicky. But Anna felt that Janek was not really talking to Nicky. He was talking to her.

'I'm off to New York tomorrow for a few days,' Janek explained. 'But when I return I should very much like it if you came for tea again. Or perhaps even dinner.'

'I'm not allowed to stay up past eight o'clock,' said Nicky.

Janek smiled. 'Then you might have to sit that one out, my little friend. Can you bear to loan me Anna for just an evening?'

'I suppose so,' said Nicky. 'She's allowed to stay up later than I am.'

'I'm glad to hear it!'

'I should have to ask Madame if it is alright,' said Anna. 'Perhaps I'll have the pleasure of meeting Miss Carmichael again.'

'Miss Carmichael? Oh, Mary. No, I doubt it. She's returned to Scotland and I don't know when she'll be visiting again.'

'Oh . . . ' Anna did not know what to say. If Janek were seeing Mary should he really be asking Anna to dinner? But of course, he only meant to invite Anna to dinner as an old friend. She would be silly to read anything else into his invitation. 'If I can get the time off, I would like it very much.'

Janek held out his hand. Balancing the cake on one of her arms, Anna gave him hers. She expected him to shake it, but instead he lifted it to his lips. Even though she wore gloves, she could feel the warmth of his mouth through the fabric, and was caught off-guard to the point that she almost dropped the cake. She just managed to rescue it before it fell to the ground.

'I'll ask the doorman to hail you a taxi,' he said, laughing. 'I don't fancy the cake's chances on the tube.'

'Oh I don't know,' said Anna, trying to calm her nerves again. 'Broken cake tastes just as good. If not better.'

'Yes it does, but does not do much for Carmichael's reputation.'

'Of course, I'm sorry.'

'I was only joking, Anna.' Janek touched her arm, then took the cake from her. 'I'll hold it until you get into the taxi.'

He waited as Anna and Nicky got into the taxi, then handed her the cake. 'Perhaps when we meet again,' he said in a low voice, 'you can tell me why there are posters in Hyde Park with your face on.'

Suddenly the sun went in for Anna, and she realised that it was probably better if she did not see Janek ever again. If he found out that not only had she harmed Teddy, but she was also a thief, he would not want anything to do with her at all.

'Anna?' Janek frowned, and stood with the door open as if waiting for an answer.

'Thank you for the lovely afternoon and for the cake,' she said, her voice trembling.

'Anna, didn't I just tell you that if you need anything you can come to me?'

'Yes, but . . . if you knew . . . '

'We'll talk about it when we meet again.' Janek shut the taxi door, and it moved away from the pavement.

Anna breathed a huge sigh of relief. She had enjoyed her afternoon with Janek and Nicky, but she decided with an aching heart that it would probably never happen again.

* * *

Teddy went upstairs to his father's room, having been told by Izzy that Sir Lionel had asked for him. Since his illness, Sir Lionel had not moved from his bedroom at all. Even though he was out of bed and sitting in a chair, he seemed to prefer the relative peace and quiet.

'Father,' said Teddy after knocking and putting his head around the door. 'Did you want me?'

'Yes, Teddy. Come in and shut the door.' Sir Lionel's chair was near the window, and he sat looking out towards the lake. 'There's a lovely view from here.'

'Why don't you come outside, Father?' asked Teddy. 'It's even nicer in the fresh air.'

'No, I like it here,' said Sir Lionel. 'Not least because your mother does not like sick rooms. She visits me in the morning to do her duty, then she leaves me to my own devices for the rest of the day. I've never read as many books as I have these past few months. Of course, young Izzy puts me through my paces in the afternoon, but I don't mind that. I find I like the girl's cheerful chatter. I gather you like her too.'

'Has she said anything?'

'No, but I see a lot from this window,' Sir Lionel said, smiling. 'Like you following her around the lake like a puppy dog.'

'I'm not a puppy!' Teddy protested.

'Oh don't take it as a criticism, boy,' said Sir Lionel. 'Every young boy needs a first love.'

Because he did not think his father

would understand, Teddy did not tell him that Izzy was his one and only love. 'Is that why you wished to see me? To talk about Izzy? Because if you tell me she's not good enough for me . . . '

Sir Lionel raised his hand. 'I intend no such thing. Not least because I know what it is to love someone whom society thinks is beneath me.'

'Mother?'

'No, not your mother. Her pedigree is impeccable. Actually that's what I wished to discuss with you.'

'Mother's pedigree?'

'No. I hear that you and Izzy are thinking of going up to see Mrs Palmer and Mr Stephens. So you can find Anna.'

'Izzy told you that?'

'Well yes. She felt she needed my permission to accompany you, what with you being under eighteen.'

'I'm quite old enough to make up my own mind.'

'Yes, I know you are, son. I've been very proud of the way you've taken the accounts in hand. I know you want to be a doctor, but I can't see that Silverton Hall would have a better master than you when I'm gone. Only . . . '

'Only what?'

'Nothing. I also gather your mother is after the combination to my safe.'

'Did Izzy tell you that too?'

'No, your mother did. She is not nearly as clever at hinting as she believes she is. The truth is, lad, that's where you come in. There is something in my safe that your mother must never see. If she does find it, she will surely destroy it. I'm not so sure I shouldn't destroy it. I find myself trapped between a rock and a hard place. But I also want to put right a dreadful wrong whilst I still have the chance.'

'How can I help, Father?'

'In my safe is a letter addressed to Anna. I want you to get it and keep it from your mother. I'm going to give you permission to look inside it. Then, if you choose to destroy it, you can. I will not hold it against you, because you're as innocent in all of this as Anna is. Or, if you wish, when you find Anna — and I pray you will find her safe and sound — you can give it to her. I'll leave it to you to decide. But you must never let your mother see it. If she finds out about it, then so be it. But if she finds it before you do, then she will most certainly destroy it.'

'Why?'

'You'll know if you choose to look inside the letter. Don't think too badly of your mother, either. Whatever she did would only be to protect you.'

'I think I can guess what the letter says,' said Teddy. 'But why now, Father? Why not when Anna first came here? Her life would have been so different.'

'Would it? I don't think so. I think it might have been worse. Mrs Palmer protected her a lot. I should have done more to take care of her; I see that now. As I said, I want to put right a dreadful wrong whilst I have the chance. This illness has made me realise I may not

140

get that chance. This is why I'm passing the baton to you. But as I said, son, I shan't think badly of you if you decide to destroy the letter. In fact I give you my permission to do so if that is your decision, as I would not have you live with the same guilty conscience as I've had to live with.'

'Father, I already feel guilty about Anna . . . '

'You shouldn't. You were just a child and your mother overruled you. She overruled me, too, when I tried to reason with her. I know it seems unlikely but I am rather afraid of Geraldine.'

'Me too. Izzy is the only one who isn't. Father?'

'Yes, Teddy?'

'If I decide to marry Izzy, neither you or Mother can change my mind.'

'Good. Good. Keep thinking that way. You'll be a much better man than I am if you learn how to stick to your guns.'

After his father told him where the

combination to the safe was hidden, with an extra warning to remove the paper taped under the desk and take it to his father for safekeeping, Teddy went downstairs to the study.

His mother was out playing bridge with friends, so hopefully would not be home until much later. Nevertheless, Teddy felt nervous about what he was about to do. Even with his father's blessing, going into Sir Lionel's safe felt like an intrusion. If his mother did return early and happened to enter the study, she would most likely demand to know what was happening.

The only thing that stopped Teddy from running out of the study and refusing to have anything to do with it was the thought that the letter for Anna might help her in some way. He owed her that much.

There was an anglepoise lamp on the desk. Teddy switched it on and pulled the drawer out, carefully removing the piece of paper so that he did not destroy the combination before he had a chance to use it. Feeling like a burglar, he knelt down by the safe and started to turn the dial, careful to turn it accurately. The first time he was so nervous, he turned it the wrong way, and did not realise until he came to open the safe only to find it still securely locked. He reminded himself that he had his father's permission, but knowing that did not stop his hands from trembling. It was not just going into his father's safe that concerned him. It was finding out the contents of the letter.

Finally, getting the combination right, the safe gave a satisfying click and the door opened when he pulled the handle. Inside the safe were several items his father had put away for safekeeping. One was an old rifle, which Teddy remembered had a faulty firing pin. He avoided that. Instead he looked through the piles of papers until he found what he was looking for: a yellowing envelope upon which was written 'For Anna'. Teddy stuffed the letter into his pocket along with the safe combination, locked the safe up firmly and turned out the lamp, before going back upstairs to his father.

'Did you get it?' asked Sir Lionel when Teddy handed him the combination.

'Yes, Father.'

'Have you opened it?'

'No, father.'

'Will you open it?'

It was something that Teddy had been considering since his father told him about the letter. He shook his head. 'No. I think I'll let Anna see it first. That would be the proper thing to do, since it's addressed to her.'

'You're not afraid of what it might say?'

'Why should I be? I know what I want to do with my life, Father, and if this letter is what I think it is, then perhaps that will make it easier for me.'

Sir Lionel was silent for a while, so Teddy took that as his cue to leave. As he was walking away, his father called him back. 'I'm very proud of you,

Teddy,' he said. 'One more thing.'

'Yes, Father?'

'If you find Anna, tell her I'd like to see her, whenever she's ready to forgive me.'

15

Anna was finding it increasingly more difficult to occupy Nicky. Every day, Madame insisted she take him out, regardless of the weather. The child really needed to be at school with other children, but Madame and Mr Voronin had insisted in hiring a private tutor for their son's education. However, as it was the summer holidays, that tutor was not due to start work until September.

She still suspected she was being got out the way for some reason and tried not to let it bother her. She felt sure that if Madame were unhappy with her, then she would say so. Similarly, if Madame had found out about what happened with Teddy, Anna would have been dismissed immediately. The Voronins took no chances with their beloved son. She was left to believe that there were just things that the Voronins and Tasha did not wish to share with her. She did wonder if it was to do with Russian state secrets, and whether they did not trust her. But many a night, Mr Voronin had talked candidly about the Russian government in her presence, so that did not seem to make sense.

To add to her somewhat gloomy mood, Janek had not contacted her again, even though it was well known that he had returned. The papers had been full of the news of the New York Carmichael's and how popular it had become in a short time. Perhaps, she thought, he felt he had done his duty in inviting an old friend for tea and did not feel the need to invite her again. Or perhaps he was spending all his time with Mary Carmichael.

'Why are you sighing?' asked Nicky as they walked through Hyde Park. If Anna had taken Nicky there in the hopes of bumping into Janek again, she had not admitted it to herself.

'Did I sigh, sweetheart? I'm sure I just took a deep breath. The air is lovely, isn't it?'

'It's all right, but it will be better at the seaside.'

'The seaside?'

'Yes, Mama said we are going there tomorrow.'

'Are we? She did not say anything to me.'

'Oh, I forgot . . . '

'Forgot what, dear?'

'It's supposed to be a secret. I'm not to tell you.'

'Oh . . . Do you mean a secret or a surprise?'

'A secret.'

'I see. Oh well, perhaps your mama and papa want time alone with you.'

'Hmm, but Tasha is coming too. I heard her talk to Mama about it. That's why Mama had to tell me. But she said I must not tell you.'

Anna swallowed hard. She must have done something to upset Madame. It was the only explanation. It was not that she expected to go on all their day trips with them; only that she always had in the past. 'I'm sure you'll have a lovely time,' she said, her voice feeling tight. 'You'll have to bring me back a stick of rock.'

'Yes, I will. And we'll send a postcard. Mama said so.'

'A postcard? For a day trip.' Anna laughed, even though there seemed to be nothing amusing about the situation to her.

'Well . . . ' said Nicky. 'It might be a bit longer than a day. I can't really remember now.' He ran on ahead, and Anna sensed that even at such a young age, he felt embarrassed by the situation. She vowed not to let it matter to her. Or at least not to let anyone see that it mattered.

'You're behaving like more of a child than Nicky,' she muttered to herself, when the feelings of disappointment and abandonment would not go away as quickly as she would have liked. Then she was able to reason it out. It was to do with cost, of course. If they took everyone from their staff, it would cost them a lot of money, and she knew that even diplomats were not terribly well paid in the Russian diplomatic service. So of course they had to be selective. Tasha had been with them longer, so she was more deserving of a trip to the seaside.

Yes, thought Anna, trying to be sensible and grown up about it, that would be the reason why. Perhaps Madame felt embarrassed about it, and that was why she had said to keep it a secret. She wished her employers had trusted her a little more, but there was nothing to be done about it.

'Come along, Nicky,' she called. 'It's time to go home.'

The following morning the family were up early, and the atmosphere in the house was very strained. They ate a virtually silent breakfast, only speaking to ask someone to pass the butter or the salt.

'Anna,' said Madame tentatively.

'Yes, Madame?'

'We are all going out today and taking Nicky with us. We thought that you have worked so hard, you deserve a day off.'

'Oh . . . thank you. That's very kind.' So that was why Madame had not invited her. She probably realised that if Anna were there, she would naturally fall into the role of caring for Nicky. It made Anna feel a little better. Madame was only thinking of her welfare. 'But I would not mind.'

'No, no, it is decided now. There is just one errand I should like you to run, if you do not mind.'

'No, not at all.'

'I have written a letter to Mr Dabrowski to thank him for the cake. I realise I should have done so weeks ago, but I have been busy with other things. There is also an invitation in there for him to come to dinner. Would you mind taking it along to him then waiting for an answer? I'll know then what to tell cook to order.'

It seemed a strange request, but Anna could do nothing but comply. 'Very well, Madame. What if Mr Dabrowski is out?'

'He is not. I checked with the hotel last night. He has been back a fortnight.'

'Oh . . . '

'Is something wrong, Anna?'

She shook her head. 'No, nothing at all.'

'He has not been in touch with you?'

'No, but he is a very busy man.'

'Of course. I just hope . . . well I hope I have not put you in an embarrassing situation.'

'No, Madame, not at all.'

'It's just that I was under the impression that you two were . . . great friends.'

'We are friends,' said Anna, blushing. 'I suppose we are, anyway.'

'Good. Good. I hope so,' Madame said, looking very worried all of a sudden.

'I'm sure he would like to come to

dinner,' said Anna hastily, afraid that she might have spoiled Madame's plans. 'What I mean is that there is no animosity between us.'

'That is comforting,' said Madame vaguely. 'Yes, very comforting.'

'Alexandra, we must be getting ready,' said Mr Voronin, looking at his watch. For a family about to spend the day at the seaside, it seemed to Anna that they were very unhappy.

'Yes of course, Yuri. Tasha, Nicky, are you ready?'

Ten minutes later, Madame and Mr Voronin, Tasha and Nicky were waiting at the front door. 'You run on ahead to Carmichael's, Anna,' Mr Voronin said in his gruff tones. 'Then the day is your own to do as you please.'

'Very well,' said Anna, once again feeling that she was being got out of the way. 'I hope you have a wonderful time at the seaside.'

'What?' Madame looked perplexed. 'Ah, I see Nicky has let you in on our little secret. We have always wanted to see the British seaside, have we not, Yuri?'

'Yes, dear, we have.'

'I'd best get going then,' said Anna, slipping between them and opening the front door.

'Anna . . . ' Madame started to speak.

'Yes, Madame?'

'We're very fond of you, child. Always remember that.'

'Alexandra,' Mr Voronin said in warning tones.

Madame glared at him, and it seemed to Anna that she was about to burst into tears. Perhaps, thought Anna, they had argued about her going with them, and it was Mr Voronin who did not want her company for the day. She did not like to think she had caused upset between a husband and wife, so she merely smiled and said, 'And I'm very fond of all of you, Madame.'

Deciding not to say anything else, for fear of adding fuel to the flames, Anna skipped down the steps, waving as she walked up the street. She was surprised to see that the Voronins and Tasha were not waving back. They simply watched her until she was out of sight.

Anna pulled her coat around her and shivered. The morning was cool, suggesting that the good days were over and autumn was just around the corner. She decided to walk to Carmichael's, even though it was across London. It would give the Voronins time to get out of the way. Then she would return and probably spend the day reading. She loved Nicky dearly, but like all children, he made great demands on her time. It would be a pleasure to sit and read a book without interruption.

With that positive thought in mind, whilst at the back of her mind was the niggling feeling that something was terribly wrong with the Voronins, she made her way to Carmichael's. It took her over an hour to get there, by which time the sun was shining high in the sky and she had to take her coat off because it was so warm.

To her surprise, Janek was standing at the entrance, and it seemed as if he was waiting for her. 'You'd better come in,' he said, before she could open her mouth to speak. 'Wait until we're in my flat upstairs before you say anything.'

Anna could only nod, dumbstruck by his attitude. For some reason it reminded her of the Voronins' mood when she had left them. 'I have a letter for you,' she said, when Janek shut the door to his flat.

'That might explain what's going on,' he said. Anna handed him the letter.

'What do you mean, what's going on?'

He put his fingers to his lips whilst he opened the letter. Inside were two notes: one for him, and one which he handed to Anna without reading.

Our dearest Anna, she read. *Please forgive us for not being honest with you. For a long time we have feared having to return to Russia. We have come to realise there is only one thing* we can do to escape that, but I am afraid it means going away to a place of safety for a long time. We thought long and hard about whether to ask you to come with us, but it seemed wrong that such a young girl should give up her freedom for us. Tasha has chosen to come with us, because she will be in danger if she does not. Please do not think badly of us for not including you in our plans. It was for your safety as much as for ours. We remain, as always your truest friends, Alexandra and Yuri Veronin.

'They've defected,' said Janek. 'Or at least they're on their way to do just that.'

'When I arrived, you said it would explain what's going on,' said Anna, feeling as if she had fallen into a deep sleep and was in the middle of a nightmare. 'What did you mean?'

'Half an hour ago all your clothes and belongings were delivered here by taxi.'

'What?' Anna put her hands to her

157

face. 'Oh, but I could have got them myself.'

'It isn't safe for you to return there, Anna. The Russian government will want to talk to everyone involved with the Voronins, including you. At least you're safe here.'

'Here? I cannot stay here,' said Anna. 'I need to go and look for a job and a place to live.'

'Then we will kill two birds with one stone. I'll give you a job and a place to stay. In fact, that's what Madame Voronin has asked me to do.'

'Oh, but you mustn't, Janek. I don't expect you to. I'll go across the road to Miss Templeton's and I'm sure she'll find me something.'

'How long is it since you've looked on the other side of this road?' Janek asked with a smile.

'I . . . I don't know.'

'Miss Templeton is not there any-more. She hasn't been for about three years. I think she married and went to live in the country. Her offices are now rented out to a firm of chartered surveyors.'

'I see . . . Well there will be other agencies.'

'Sit down, Anna and I'll get you a cup of tea. You look unwell.' When she did not comply, Janek said in firmer tones. 'Sit down, Anna.'

Like a child, she obeyed him, sitting down on the plush leather sofa. It was just as well, because her legs had been about to give way. 'I knew something was wrong,' she said, in a daze. 'Why could they not trust me?'

'I've told you, they knew that you'd be questioned.'

'I would never have betrayed them.'

'Anna, I'm not talking about before they defected, but after. You don't know much about the Russian authorities, but I can tell you that I do. They are ruthless. Madame Voronin did the only thing she could do to protect you. She kept you in the dark, and then she sent you to someone whom she knew would take care of you. Probably because I had before.'

'I don't need to be taken care of,' Anna said with uncharacteristic petulance. 'I'm not a ten-year-old girl anymore, Janek.' She immediately regretted her outburst, but her sadness over losing a family she had come to think of as her own had made her tetchy. Even though she understood that the Voronins had not meant it that way, she could not help feeling hurt that they had not trusted her. She could at least have made her own arrangements about where to live and work, rather than have them rely on the kindness of Janek. It embarrassed her that once again she was seeking his help.

'Strange,' said Janek. 'I'd have sworn from the look on your face that you were still running away from something.'

16

On the morning that the Voronins defected, Teddy and Izzy had really gone to the seaside. It was a long trip from Surrey to the East Yorkshire coast, so most of the day had been spent travelling by train. They booked into the first bed and breakfast establishment they found, deciding to begin their search for Mrs Palmer and Mr Stephens on the following morning. They had no idea where Mrs Palmer and her sister had set up their hotel, as Teddy had not heard from them since the day they left Silverton Hall. He only knew that it was definitely in Filey.

Teddy thought they might get lucky by asking the landlady of the place in which they stayed. 'Do you happen to know of a bed and breakfast place run by two sisters?' he asked the landlady as they booked in. 'Mrs Palmer and

. . . Oh what was the other one's name? I know her first name was Elsie.'

The landlady, who introduced herself as Mrs Green, sniffed. 'Deciding to move on already, are you?' she said.

'Oh no,' said Izzy hastily. 'They're old friends of ours and we just thought we might pop in.'

'Seems to me,' said Mrs Green, 'that if they're old friends, you'd know where you are.' Her eyes narrowed. 'Are you two married?'

'No,' said Izzy firmly. 'This is why we're booking separate rooms.'

'Well, just be aware that we want no funny business. This is a respectable establishment. Door's locked at nine pm, so make sure you return on time if you go out this evening. I don't make allowances. Breakfast is at eight am on the dot — not a minute earlier, not a minute later. If you miss it, you look like eating out. And don't come down early because you'll be in the way. No smoking in the bedrooms.'

'We don't smoke,' said Teddy. 'It's

bad for your health.'

'And no cooking in the bedrooms either,' Mrs Green snapped, ignoring him.

It was a struggle for them not to giggle as they were shown to their rooms. 'I've heard of prisons that were more welcoming than this,' Izzy muttered to Teddy as they climbed the stairs. After that he dared not look at her, in case he burst out laughing.

After a good night's sleep, they sat down to a rather insipid breakfast, which was lukewarm at best. The other guests in the dining room sat staring into space as they ate, it being clear that Mrs Green did not tolerate noise or frivolity of any kind. One young couple had a job keeping their toddler quiet. Regardless of the tense atmosphere, the little girl insisted on having the time of her life. Other guests smiled indulgently, probably wishing they could join in, but with one eye on the door in case the harridan Mrs Green should return.

'I'm surprised she's still in business,' said Teddy.

'Maybe they're like us,' said Izzy. 'Came here direct from the train and have regretted it since. She probably won't let anyone leave. We'll all be trapped here forever, eating soggy bacon and not daring to make a noise.'

Teddy coughed to hide another fit of giggles. Izzy's pretty green eyes shone, and he noticed her shoulders shaking. 'Even this place is fun with you, Izzy,' he said.

'Yes, I'm having a good time too, Teddy. Shall we leave this awful breakfast and go to the Brontë Vinery instead?'

'The Brontë Vinery?'

'Yes, it's a lovely café in Cliff House, where the Brontës used to come and stay. They do a great breakfast which you eat sitting under the vines.'

'Really?' Teddy lowered his voice. 'I'd have sworn from reading all that misery in Wuthering Heights that they stayed here.'

'Shh . . . ' Izzy's lips twisted as she tried to contain her laughter. 'We'd better go before we get in trouble.'

'Where are you going?' asked Mrs Green as they made their escape from the dining room.

'We're going in search of our friends,' said Teddy.

'You've not finished your breakfast. That's waste that is. How am I supposed to make a living here if people waste their food?'

'We paid you for it,' said Izzy.

'Of course,' said Mrs Green, 'you youngsters have soon forgotten the war, and the sacrifices we had to make. When there was rationing, no one wasted anything. Never mind. If you don't eat it today, we'll warm it up for you tomorrow.'

'She has a point, you know,' said Teddy when they were walking along the seafront ten minutes later. 'It was wrong to waste food.'

'Yes, I suppose it was,' said Izzy. 'But it was inedible, Teddy. I've got a tummy ache even from the bit I did eat.'

'Yes, me too. I don't know if I want to eat anything else at the moment.'

'No, me neither. We'll put off the vinery for another day. Let's go and look for Mrs Palmer. With any luck we'll find her and she'll have rooms we can stay in.'

'There's no rush, really,' said Teddy. 'The longer we're here, the longer I get to spend with you.'

'Some of us have to work for a living.'

'I suppose you think I'm a poor little rich boy,' said Teddy, sulking. 'I can't help the life I was born into, Izzy, but I want to make things better. I want to help others. Can't you at least give me credit for that?'

'Hey, I was teasing. You're all right, Teddy. One of the good guys, as they say in American films.'

Teddy smiled, very quickly mollified. 'So there's a chance for me yet then?'

'If you mean to do great things in the world, yes. If you mean with me . . . I've told you before, Teddy, I think you're a lovely lad, but you're three years younger than me, and still at school. Come back when you're a bit more grown up.'

'That's as good as a promise. Unless of course you fall hopelessly in love with someone else by then.'

'I'm afraid that's something you'll have to be prepared for. I don't say it to be unkind, Teddy, so please don't look so crestfallen. I say it out of kindness. Because it's just as likely you'll find a girl and completely forget about me. This is the way it should be at your age.'

'You talk as if you're years older than I am, but as you said yourself, it's three years.'

'I feel older. Girls always mature quicker than boys. You've still a lot of growing up to do.'

'The thing is, you're always going to be three years older than me. So in three years' time when I'm nineteen, you'll be twenty-two, and you'll still say I'm too young. Perhaps you're right;

perhaps it's best if we remain friends and that I don't build my hopes up. All I can say at the moment is that being with you makes me happier than I've ever been. You talk to me as an equal. The same way Anna used to talk to me, in fact. Mother and Father always talk down to me, whilst others are deferential because of my upbringing. I don't much like either. You can scoff and call me 'poor little rich boy' if you like, but it's the truth. I'm just a normal human being like everyone else and I want to be around people who treat me that way.'

'I shan't scoff again, I promise,' said Izzy. 'I honestly can't think of a better friend to have, Teddy.' She slipped her arm in his. 'Come on, let's go and find Mrs Palmer and Mr Stephens. With any luck we'll walk off that breakfast and be ready for something decent to eat.'

They started walking the length of the sea front, going into each guest-house along the way and asking for Mrs Palmer and Mr Stephens. As with the landlady at the guesthouse in which they were staying, the owners were a little unhelpful. They stopped long enough to eat a lunch of fish and chips as they sat on the sands. A bracing breeze from the North Sea whipped at their faces, but as the sun shone above, it was not too cold. The sea breeze and the tangy aroma of vinegar made their mouths water even as they ate. The unpleasant breakfast was quickly forgotten, replaced by the delicious taste of cod and chips.

'This is the best food I've ever tasted,' said Teddy. 'Who knew eating out of newspaper could be so delicious?'

'Half the population actually,' said Izzy, chewing a juicy chip. 'Fish and chips are so good for the soul. It's part of being British.'

'I've certainly never felt so British.'

When Izzy had finished her food, she spread out the newspaper. 'I like to see what was happening yesterday,' she said, smiling. It was a local newspaper, full of Filey news. She perused the greasy pages whilst Teddy finished his food.

'Teddy, look!' she exclaimed.

'What? What's wrong?'

'Nothing! Look, there's an article here about a hotel called Anna's Return. It won an award for excellence from the local council.'

'So?'

Izzy looked at him as if he were particularly stupid. 'What is your half-sister's name?'

Teddy's eyes lit up. 'Anna. Surely you don't think it's Mrs Palmer's? It would be too easy.'

'Don't you think it's a bit of a coincidence? The rest of the article is missing, so it doesn't say who owns the hotel and there's no address, but I reckon if we ask around we'll find out easily enough. We should go there. We've nothing to lose.'

'You're right,' said Teddy. He stood up and screwed his chip wrappings into a ball, in order to throw it in the nearest waste bin. 'We'll go there. If it turns out to be the right place, we won't be wandering around aimlessly all day.'

Izzy ripped out the bit of paper from the sheet and screwed up the rest. 'We'd best clean up first,' she said to Teddy after they had put the paper into the bin. She held up her ink-blackened hands. 'The only problem with yesterday's news is yesterday's newsprint.'

Anna's Return was on a quiet side street of Filey, rather than on the sea front. It looked welcoming even from the outside, with whitewashed walls and pretty curtains in the window. What was more, the holidaymakers coming out through the front door were smiling and looking back, seemingly engaging in chatter with someone inside.

'I can't imagine Mrs Green allowing all that happiness,' said Izzy.

'Goodness no,' said Teddy. 'It would lower the tone of the place.'

If Teddy hoped to see Mrs Palmer on reception, he was to be disappointed. The desk clerk was a young man in his

171

thirties with an open smile and charming disposition. His nametag said he was called Richard Preston. 'Can I be of assistance?' he asked Teddy and Izzy.

'Actually we're looking for an old friend of mine,' said Teddy. 'A Mrs Palmer?'

'Is she a guest here?' Richard asked.

'No, oh . . . I thought she might be the owner,' said Teddy. 'I'm sorry. I think we've wasted your time.'

'Just a minute,' said Izzy, stopping Teddy as he was about to turn and leave. 'What about a Mr Stephens? Is he here?'

'I'm afraid my uncle, Mr Stephens, has gone to the cash and carry,' said Richard. 'He'll be back in about an hour. My aunt, Mrs Stephens, is in. Would you like to speak to her?'

'Yes, yes, we would,' said Izzy.

'Wait one moment. I'll just go and fetch her.'

'It can't be the same Mr Stephens,' said Teddy, when Richard had gone into a room marked private. 'He was supposed to live with Mrs Palmer.'

'Well if he met someone else and married, I'd imagine he'd live with her instead,' said Izzy. 'They should be able to tell us where Mrs Palmer is.'

'Yes, you're right.'

The door to the private room opened and a woman stood in the doorway.

'Mrs Stephens?' said Izzy, stepping forward.

'No, it's Mrs Palmer!' Teddy exclaimed, his face breaking into a huge grin.

Mrs Palmer frowned. 'It's Mrs Stephens nowadays. How can I . . . ' She stopped and looked more closely at Teddy. 'It can't be. Can it? It's not Master Edward?'

'The one and only,' said Teddy. 'Oh Mrs. Palmer . . . sorry, Mrs Stephens. You don't know how happy I am to see you at last! Izzy, this is her. This is our old housekeeper.'

'I think I'd worked that one out,' said Izzy with a smile.

17

'I think it might be less confusing if you called me Polly,' said Mrs Stephens. She had taken Teddy and Izzy into the private room, which turned out to be a neat and homely sitting room with a desk at one end, covered in accounts and other papers. She asked Richard to bring tea and biscuits. 'And is this your young lady, Master Edward?'

'We're just friends,' said Teddy, blushing.

'I'm Isobel McDonald. Izzy to my friends. I'm a nurse to Sir Lionel.'

'I'm very glad to meet you, Izzy. I'm sorry to hear Sir Lionel has been unwell. Is that why you've come to me, Master Edward? Because I can't return now, even if I wanted to.'

'No, that's not why. Father is making a vast improvement, and we keep getting staff from an agency. None of them stay very long.'

'So not much has changed then,' said Polly, pursing her lips.

'I had no idea that you and Mr Stephens had married.'

'Well we always talked about it, you know.'

'No, I didn't know,' said Teddy. 'You kept it hidden well.' As far as he could remember, things had been rather strained between Mr Stephens and Mrs Palmer, with each fighting for supremacy over the domestic arrangements at Silverton. At the very least, Mrs Palmer always seemed cross with Mr Stephens. Perhaps that was how love manifested itself for some people.

'Then when we came here, Horace almost fell foul of the residency laws, so I said we might as well get married. That way he couldn't be thrown out on the street after twenty-eight days.'

Richard came back into the room with a tray of tea and cakes. 'This is Richard Preston,' said Polly. 'He's Horace's nephew and the best desk clerk in the world. Richard, this is young Master Edward Silverton who I told you about, and his friend, Izzy.'

'I'm glad to meet you both,' said Richard, smiling. 'Aunt Polly has lots of tales of her life at Silverton Hall. She always speaks well of you and your . . .' Richard paused, as if afraid he had spoken out of turn. 'Young Anna.'

'It's alright, you can say she's my sister,' said Teddy. 'I'm very proud of the fact. Actually we've come to see you about her.' He looked at Polly. 'I heard that you tried to find her and wondered if you'd been successful.'

Polly shook her head sadly. 'No. We put up posters in London in the area where she posted the letter to Horace from. But we've heard nothing. I can only hope and pray that she's safe. I thought we'd call the guesthouse *Anna's Return*, so that if she ever came looking for us, she'd know where to find us. Silly I suppose.'

'Not silly at all. The thing is,' said Teddy, 'I've got a letter to her from

Father, and he would like to see her too.'

Polly sniffed and made a harrumph sound in her throat. 'Pity he didn't think of that when the poor little mite was living in his house, forced to be a servant. I'm sorry, Master Edward, I shouldn't speak out of turn . . . '

'Why not?' said Izzy. 'You're in your own house now. You can say what you wish.'

Polly looked at Izzy with admiration. 'Are you sure you're not his young lady? You'd be very good for him. A man needs a woman who can manage him, and don't you ever let them tell you any different. Why, Horace seems ten years younger since we opened the guesthouse.'

'Is your sister still with you?' asked Teddy.

'No. We had a parting of the ways,' said Polly stiffly. 'We started a guest-house together, but disagreed over how it should be run. She wanted it like an army camp and I think that people come on holiday to relax. Then she took up with some man who almost brought us all to ruin. Horace and I were going to move back down south, but as luck would have it, this came up, and we decided to try our luck. Things seem to be going well. Which is more than I can say for Dunromin', or Dunsmiling as we call my sister's place.'

'That's where we're staying,' said Izzy.

'Mrs Green?' said Teddy, wide-eyed. 'Your sister is Mrs Green?'

'Yes, that's our Elsie.'

'But she said she didn't know you,' Izzy said.

'Well she would, wouldn't she? We don't talk anymore. I'm only glad young Anna didn't come here, or Elsie would have worked her even harder than she had to work at Silverton Hall. She doesn't treat her staff or her guests right, and that's a fact. I can't believe you're staying there.'

'We were,' said Teddy, 'but if you have two rooms going spare . . . '

'Of course I have, and you don't have to pay either.'

'Now Polly,' said Izzy, 'you can't run a business like that. We'll pay our way.'

'You're a good girl,' said Polly, looking from Izzy to Teddy then back again. 'Yes, I think you'll do quite nicely for him, regardless of what you say about only being friends.'

'So,' said Teddy, grinning at Izzy. 'Which one of us is going to tell Mrs Green we're not stopping another night?'

'You're the one who wants to prove you're grown up,' said Izzy, with a wink at Polly Stephens.

Teddy and Izzy spent a happy couple of days with Polly and Mr Stephens, before returning home to tell his father that Anna had not yet been found.

18

'Anna, we have another problem with the laundry,' said Florentyna, stepping into Anna's office.

'Oh no. What now?'

'These sheets are barely clean.' Florentyna held up one to show. The sheet, though pressed, still looked grubby.

'I'll get on to them. Do we have enough to change all the beds?'

Florentyna nodded. 'Yes, don't worry. Some rooms were empty last night, so we can leave those sheets on, can't we? I know it's not policy . . .'

'But it's common sense,' said Anna, smiling. 'They won't be dirty. Just give the top covers a good shake to get rid of any dust that might have settled. Do you want me to help?'

'Oh you're far too important to change beds now,' said Florentyna with a wink.

Anna blushed. She had only been working at Carmichael's for two years, but when the previous housekeeper had left to have a baby, Janek had insisted she take the role. 'You should not be changing beds anyway,' he had said to her. As always, Anna argued that she was quite capable of hard work, but Janek insisted she had done enough of that in her life. 'You've earned a promotion,' he had said. 'Maybe not here, but with all those years you spent at Silverton Hall.'

'I'm still happy to help, Florentyna,' Anna said earnestly.

'I know. I'm just teasing. If I had your head for figures, I'd probably be housekeeper by now.'

'I could put in a word with Mr Dabrowski.'

'No, please don't. Really, I'm happy not to have the responsibility. Neither do I fancy having to deal with that harridan at the laundry.'

'We should really have our own by now,' said Anna. 'I'm sure we could utilise a few rooms in the basement. It would create more jobs too.' She made a note to mention it to Janek when they had their next meeting.

When that would be, she did not know. He was away a lot, visiting the other hotels, and overseeing the building of a new Carmichael's in Washington. In a lot of ways, Anna felt sad that her job at Carmichael's had turned their relationship to a professional footing. It seemed to her that they could not be friends, not whilst he employed her. It was bad enough to hear the whispers of the other staff, some of whom were less gracious than Florentyna about Anna's quick promotion to housekeeper.

'I'll get in touch with the laundrette,' she said to Florentyna.

As her friend turned to leave, Anna called her back.

'Who was on desk duty and room service last night, Florentyna? Do you know?'

'Er, yes, I think it was Reg Turner on

182

the desk, and Vince O'Brian on room service. Why?' Florentyna's eyes became watchful. Anna remembered that Florentyna had a bit of a thing going with Reg Turner.

'Oh it's just that one of the guests complained to me as they were coming out of their room this morning, and said that they ordered a bottle of whisky last night, but when it came it tasted watered down.'

'Would that be Major Dalrymple?'

'Yes, that's him.'

'He always says that. Every time he stays. It's my guess that he's drunk so much of it over the years, it's ruined his taste buds.'

Anna laughed. 'Yes, I'm sure you're right. Still, I'll have a word with Reg and Vince just so they can be aware of the complaint.'

'Anna?' Florentyna hesitated, as if there was something she wanted to say but was not sure if she should.

'Hmm?'

'Sometimes it's best just to let these

little complaints go. It's not worth upsetting anyone.'

'I wasn't going to discipline Reg and Vince,' said Anna. 'It's not even my job to do so. I just thought I'd mention it, in case the Major makes a formal complaint. Tip them off, sort of thing.'

'Oh. So you . . . er . . . you wouldn't be upset if it was watered down whisky then?'

Anna's eyes widened in surprise. 'Of course I would be. As I'm sure Mr Dabrowski would. Carmichael's has a name for excellence. Serving our customers watered-down drinks would not only sully that name, but . . . well it is illegal, isn't it?'

'Yes, I suppose so.'

'Florentyna, if there's something you know . . . '

'No,' Florentyna said vehemently. 'No, of course not. I was just wondering about your opinion of it, that's all.'

'Testing me?'

Florentyna laughed. 'I should have known better than to even try. You're

184

whiter than white, Anna. Always have been.'

When Florentyna left, Anna frowned. Had Janek set up that test for her? To ensure she was trustworthy? If so, why would he do such a thing?

Since she started working for Janek, he had not mentioned seeing her face on flyers in Hyde Park, for which she was thankful. It seemed to Anna that keeping her job at Carmichael's relied on him not thinking that she was either capable of harming a child or of theft. She had lived so long with the shame of both, that she had lost her sense of perspective about it all. As each year passed and she kept her secret, her shame became weightier and her fear of being found out immense. Especially of being found out by Janek, whose good opinion she valued more than anyone's.

But what if he had found out? He only need make enquiries at Silverton Hall, and he would quite easily learn what had happened. Anna had no doubt that her step-mother would be falling over herself to tell him. It might explain Florentyna's trap. If indeed it was a trap.

An hour later, after she had finished her paperwork for the morning, and with her head clearer, Anna began to wonder more at Florentyna's question. She knew Florentyna was honest, but that did not mean that Reginald Turner was as reliable. Reg had come to the hotel soon after it opened, as an ex-soldier injured in the war. He walked with a limp and carried a walking stick, which was almost his trademark. The guests liked him for his easy charm and good looks (and Florentyna agreed with them!) but also because he was a *bona fide* war hero. Not that he talked about it. He would always dismiss any questions as to how he became injured with a wave of his hand. 'It was nothing. I did no more than anyone else out there,' he would say, whilst shaking his head sagely. This only made people like him more.

Vincent O'Brian was around Reg's

age, but had not fought in the war on account of coming from southern Ireland. Like Reg, he was a good looking, charming young man, and even more attractive to the female guests because of his soft Irish lilt, which he used to good effect to charm them all. It was sometimes a bone of contention amongst the room service staff that Vince's tips were always bigger than anyone else's. But he was a generous lad, and spent most of his money on buying the others' drinks, so they quickly forgot about their jealousy until the next time Vince had a big tip.

The two young men were often seen together after work, going to the local pubs, before coming back to the bedroom which they shared at the back of the hotel. If anyone kept the staff awake at night by laughing and singing, it was most likely to be Reg and Vince. But it was an unwritten rule that one did not tell on one's workmates, so they got away with a lot.

What, thought Anna, if they thought

they could get away with even more? She felt guilty for distrusting them. Neither had been anything other than polite to her since she arrived. It was only one complaint after all, and from a man who was known to spend most of his life drunk.

Nevertheless, she had the hotel to think about. Janek had placed great trust in her. Anna was acutely aware that not all the staff were as easy-going as Florentyna about her being promoted to housekeeper so quickly. It put pressure on her to earn her place in the role.

Thinking carefully about how she might word the complaint to the two young men, Anna went downstairs to the foyer. Reg was on the desk, dealing with two new guests who had come to the hotel for lunch. They were a young man and woman in their early twenties. The girl was particularly noticeable, with glorious auburn hair and pretty freckles. The young man was studious-looking, with thick horn-rimmed glasses.

As always, Reg Turner was charm personified. 'And if there's anything you need, Mr. Harrington, you only need to ask. We aim to please at Carmichael's.'

'Thank you,' said the young man. 'Of course, I've been here plenty of times, but it's Miss McDonald's first time. Isn't it, Isobel?'

'Yes, I've always wanted to come here,' said the young woman. Her voice had a warm Scottish lilt, yet she seemed ill at ease in her surroundings. Just as Anna had been the first time she had stepped into Carmichael's. Even though Anna did not know the girl, she warmed to her as a kindred spirit.

'Well, Miss, you have a good time, and tell all your friends about Carmichael's.'

'Oh I'll be sending out hundreds of letters to tell everyone I know that I visited.' Miss McDonald smiled.

The girl and her male friend turned to go into the restaurant, and it was then that the girl saw Anna. She stopped dead, to the point that the couple behind who were moving towards the reception desk almost bumped into her. 'Sorry,' the girl said with a shy smile.

'Come along, Isobel,' said Harrington, sounding peeved. 'Really, there's no need to be quite so nervous.'

'No, it's not that,' said Isobel as he drew her away. 'I just thought I saw . . . ' Her voice trailed away as they entered the bustling dining room.

Anna waited until Reg was free and asked him to accompany her to the back office.

'Is something wrong, Anna?' he asked.

'Oh no,' she said with a smile, hoping he would not see how worried she really was. 'It's just that . . . well I wondered if Major Dalrymple made a complaint to you this morning.'

'Old Dalrymple? I don't think so. Why?'

'He said something to me about his whisky tasting watered down.'

'I'd be surprised if he could tell, the

amount he drinks,' said Reg, laughing. Anna laughed too, but she was still troubled. That was pretty much what Florentyna had said. Almost as if it had been rehearsed.

'You're probably right,' said Anna. 'I wouldn't like to think the supplier was shortchanging us though.' She had decided on that explanation for her concern on the way downstairs. That way it did not seem as if she were accusing anyone in the hotel.

'I'll keep an eye on the situation,' said Reg. 'It might have been just a bad batch.'

'Yes, I'm sure that's all it was. I thought I'd mention it.'

'Of course, Anna. You did the right thing. We want to keep the guests happy here, don't we?'

She agreed with a smile. Reg returned to his work, and Anna took a moment to compose herself. She was surprised to realise she felt great relief that things had not been worse. Reg might have taken umbrage at her question, and with good reason if he were totally innocent.

She decided to take a walk. She had been cooped up in the hotel for too long, and needed some fresh air.

19

'So,' said George Harrington, 'what do you want to eat, Isobel? My treat. Isobel?'

Izzy was not listening. The dining room was only separated from the foyer by a large archway, and it was through this archway that Izzy was looking, hoping to catch a glimpse of the beautiful dark-haired girl again. She was sure it was Teddy's sister — the girl certainly looked similar to the one in Teddy's photograph — but had been too shy to ask. That was partly due to the surroundings, and partly due to her nerves over being asked out by George Harrington. Besides one did not go up to complete strangers and ask if they were the runaway sister of one's friend.

Izzy thought George would never ask her out, but now that he had, she was not exactly enjoying the experience.

The scene at the desk had been a case in point. Did he have to tell the whole world that she was not used to dining in style? Or that by comparison he was very practised in the art? It had been much the same all morning. They had gone to the National Gallery, where he had patronised her repeatedly about the artwork on show. At one point she had snapped, 'George, I may be from the poor side of Edinburgh but I do know a Van Gogh when I see one.'

She could not help thinking that Teddy would never treat her in such a way. Even though he was the son of a knight, he had always talked to Izzy as an equal. Or mostly in a way that suggested he thought her better than he was. This was rather sweet really.

She had not seen him since their trip to Filey. As soon as they returned, he had gone back to boarding school and Izzy's services as a nurse were no longer needed at Silverton Hall on account of Sir Lionel's health improving. That was over two years ago, and she was forced to admit that she missed his friendship. And his dog-like devotion, she thought with a wry grin. There was something rather nice about being adored. No doubt, all these months later, he would be showing the same dog-like devotion to a girl at school. Izzy did not know why this should bother her. He was probably still too young for her, even though he would be over eighteen by now. They had written to each other a few times, but their worlds seemed to have diverged somewhat.

'Are you with me or not, Isobel?' George said with a sigh.

'I'm sitting here, aren't I?' she said, brightly. But just at that moment, the pretty dark-haired girl came out of the office and went out through the front door. Izzy feared she might have lost her. If she had been a guest who called in briefly to make a complaint then she might not return that day, and Izzy had no idea where to start looking. 'Excuse me one minute, George,' she said, coming to a decision.

Izzy got up and went to the reception desk. 'Excuse me.'

'Yes, what can I do to help you, Miss?' The desk clerk asked. He was a handsome young man, and his name on his lapel said 'Reginald Turner'.

'I wondered. That girl. The really pretty one with dark hair. Her name is not Anna Silverton, is it?'

A cloud passed over the man's eyes, and he seemed to undergo some thought process, albeit very quickly. 'No, that's Miss Palmer.'

'Oh right,' said Izzy, feeling sure he had lied for some reason. There was something about his manner that seemed strange. But it was not as if he were protecting the dark-haired girl. Far from it. Izzy could not put her finger on it, but it felt very much as if he was storing the information about the name Anna Silverton away for some other purpose.

Realising she was behaving like a character in a spy novel, Izzy smiled and said, 'Sorry to bother you. Thank you.'

It was only an hour later, when she and George were saying a strained goodbye on Tower Bridge, that she remembered that Teddy's ex-housekeeper Mrs Stephens used to be called Mrs Palmer, and she and Anna were very close. What better name to use than Anna Palmer?

When George had gone, Izzy stood on Tower Bridge for a while, trying to decide what to do. She thought about telephoning Teddy at the teaching hospital in Wales where he was training to be a doctor. She knew from his letters that he had fought something of a battle with his mother, who tried to insist that if he was to be a doctor, he should at least attend Oxford or Cambridge and become a physician of great renown, perhaps even tending the Queen and her family. Teddy had refused, saying that to go to either university meant three years of degree work before he even got to see a real patient. He wanted to be at the forefront of medicine, he had told Izzy in a letter, not taking care of spoiled rich women who suffered with nervous tension. 'I want to help those who genuinely need it,' he said.

Izzy looked inside herself and asked a searching question. Did she want to telephone Teddy to tell him she may have seen his sister? Or did she want to telephone him because she missed his friendship and wanted to hear his voice again? Sighing, she stood looking out over the Thames. Perhaps both were valid reasons. After all, if it was Anna that she saw, he would want to know. But what about after she had told him? What then? Would he just thank her and put the phone down? Or would he want to see her? And if he did not ask to see her, how might she feel?

'Oh you're an idiot, Izzy,' she told herself. 'Two years ago he was yours for the taking, but oh no, you had to be the sensible one.' Not that she would have done things differently. He was only sixteen at the time. 'Right,' she said, not noticing the funny looks from people who saw her talking to herself, 'I'll telephone him and not expect anything else. That would be the proper thing. He would want to know about his sister.'

She managed to find a few coins and a phone box. She had the number of Teddy's halls of residence in her handbag. It was only when she was halfway through dialling the number that it occurred to her he might not even be there. He could be in class. Or out with his friends. Or out with another girl. 'Get a grip, Izzy,' she muttered, as the sound of ringing started in the earpiece.

Of course, Teddy was not the one who answered, and there was an agonising wait whilst the young man who did answer went in search of him. As it turned out there was very little money left in the phone by the time Teddy did answer.

'Hello?'

'Teddy, it's Izzy. This'll have to be quick. I'm in London and I think I've just seen Anna . . . ' It was at that point the line went dead.

20

Janek watched Anna from his balcony, her glossy black hair shining in the morning sunlight as she walked back to the hotel. He had returned whilst she was out walking, and his first thought on arriving back at Carmichael's had been of seeing her. In fact, his thoughts all the time he was away were of Anna.

Despite his pleasure at seeing her again, he was troubled. There had been no question that he would help Anna when the Voronins asked him two years earlier. He would never see her out on the streets, and she had been so dazed by the sudden defection of people she thought of as family, he had been afraid she would not be able to focus on finding somewhere else quickly. Thankfully for her peace of mind, the Voronins had written to her from exile as soon as they could, asking her forgiveness. Being the girl she was, she forgave them without question.

'It must have been so hard for them, worrying all the time about being sent back to Russia,' she confided in Janek. 'I thought it was just . . . oh a ghost story . . . like tales of the bogeyman. I had no idea just how terrified they were. They liked living in the West with all the freedom that entailed, and I think they wanted Nicky to grow up in a free country.'

'It is difficult to completely give up your home,' Janek said, with fellow feeling for the Voronins. With the situation as it was in Poland, he could not return either and wondered if he ever might. 'It was a very brave decision for them. I hope they find the freedom they craved.'

Once she had heard from her friends, Anna settled into working at Carmichael's better. Janek suspected that for a while she waited for a call from them, to tell her it had all been a mistake and she could return to her job. Even though Janek knew it was rather selfish of him, he was relieved when they did not.

But he had inadvertently made things strained between himself and Anna. He knew that the rest of the staff gossiped about her relatively quick promotion to housekeeper. As far as Janek was concerned, she deserved the job, and she was very good at it, but others did not see it that way. Therefore, he did not want to fuel that fire by being seen talking to her too often. He did not much care about his own reputation — he was worldly wise enough to realise that men were never totally ruined by gossip in the way women were. But he cared deeply about Anna's reputation. He knew how cruel the world could be about successful, intelligent women.

That did not solve the problem of how he could spend time with her without inciting gossip, which was something he dearly wanted to do. Her blossoming, which had begun under the

care of Madame Voronin, had continued during her time at Carmichael's.
She had become a confident young
woman, which only added to her
beauty. But she was also kind and
thoughtful. Even the staff who gossiped
about her could not put their hands on
their hearts and say they did not like
her.

'Oh just ask her,' he muttered to
himself. 'Never mind what others
think.' Except he did mind, for her
sake.

'Talking to yourself, darling?' said a
voice from behind him. It was Mary
Carmichael. Janek was struck by how
very hard Mary tried to look attractive,
compared to Anna who hardly tried at
all, and yet was ten times lovelier. He
pushed the unkind thought aside. It was
not Mary's fault she was not Anna.

'Mary! I didn't hear you arrive.'

'I wanted to surprise you, darling.'
Mary threw her coat over the back of a
chair and sat down at the patio table.
'Scotland was so boring without you,

and you never come up to see us anymore.'

Janek smiled. 'Mike may sleep as much as he likes in this partnership. Unfortunately I have to work.'

'You work too hard. Everyone says so, including my brother. This is why I've come down to rescue you. What about a show, and dinner afterwards? Dancing even. You remember how to dance, don't you?'

'Vaguely.'

'Do you remember how to kiss?' Mary crossed her legs in a sultry fashion.

'I thought we agreed, Mary . . . Or at least you did. You had other fish to fry.' There was nothing bitter about the way Janek spoke. In fact he smiled indulgently as he said it. He was well aware of Mary's fickle nature, and did not resent his part as of one of her flash-in-the pan love affairs.

'Oh that was then. I've made a dreadful mistake, darling. Can we try again?'

'No, things have changed. I've changed, Mary.'

'So I've heard. The staff here do like to gossip, you know.'

Janek's smile faded. 'Really?'

'Yes, about you and the housekeeper. She's that girl you escaped from France with, isn't she? The one we met in Hyde Park, with that funny little Russian boy. Honestly darling, it's very naughty, fraternising with the staff. You must know that.'

'I am aware of that,' said Janek, biting down the anger he felt about Mary pinpointing his own concerns. It only proved to him that he was right to keep Anna at a distance. He hated the idea of people talking about her in such a way. 'The staff — and you — have got it entirely wrong. Me and Anna are friends, nothing more. So perhaps the next time you join in the gossip, you could add that to the story.'

'Oh now you're sulking and you'll be no good to me whatsoever. I'm going shopping.' Mary stood up, smiling smugly. Janek had the distinct impression that Mary's plan, whatever it was, had worked. 'Let me know about dinner and a show later, when you've made up your mind. Hmm?'

Janek was about to ask her what she meant by 'made up your mind' but he already knew Mary was not really talking about dinner and a show. It was possible that Mary only wanted him because she thought she could not have him.

At that moment it seemed as if a cloud passed in front of the sun, and a shiver trickled down his spine. Mary was a nice enough girl most of the time, but she did not like to be thwarted in love. If she had made up her mind to have him, then she intended it to happen. She might even add fuel to the flames of gossip running around the hotel. He had no choice but to keep his relationship with Anna on a purely professional footing. Gossip was bad enough. But Mary's claws were sharper than any of the staff's tongues, and he did not want Anna to be wounded by her.

His decision meant that when he went to Anna's office later that day, he was much cooler with her than he intended to be.

'How are things?' he asked. 'No problems with the staff?'

'No problems at all. They're very good staff, Jan . . . Mr Dabrowski,' said Anna, who always reverted to his formal name when they talked business. She looked bemused. Normally he asked about her first, and then the business. Despite her answer, he sensed she was holding something back.

'If there's anything I should know . . .'

'No, nothing at all. I'll come to you if there are any problems.'

'Very well. Don't let me keep you from your work any longer.'

It felt to Janek as though an eight-foot-high glass wall had been erected between them. He told himself as he left her office that he was doing it to protect her. But part of him wondered how much he was guarding his own heart against being hurt. He had lost everyone he loved before the war, and despite his success and the fact that if anyone asked him he would have said he was happy, he had a deep-seated fear of losing another loved one. Perhaps that was why he had avoided falling in love. He thought of Anna, looking bemused in her office, and knew that he had already failed to keep his heart safe.

21

Anna could not help wondering what she might have done to annoy Janek. He had seemed very tense when he came to see her. Was it possible that Dalrymple had complained to him and he thought she was neglecting her duties by not mentioning it?

She struggled to concentrate on her work for the rest of the day. Perhaps she should say something? She had not yet spoken to Vince O'Brian. He might be able to shed light on it. The more Anna thought about it, the more she hated mistrusting her work colleagues. She knew what it was to be falsely accused, and she could not bear the thought of making someone else feel the pain of suspicion.

'You're lost in thought, so you are,' said Vince O'Brian from her office doorway. She was surprised to see him.

It was about five o'clock and he was not due to start his shift until eight.

'Vince! I was just thinking about you.'

'I'm very glad to hear it,' he said with a smile. Vince often tried to flirt with Anna, but she just laughed it off. He flirted with everyone.

'Not you personally.' She quickly explained about Major Dalyrymple's complaint. 'I was afraid the supplier might be watering down the whisky,' she added hastily.

'I'll keep an eye on it,' said Vince. 'I came to tell you that me, Reg and Florentyna are off out for a pub meal until the evening shift. We wondered if you'd like to come.'

Anna shook her head. 'Sorry, I've loads to do here. I've barely caught up today.'

'You work too hard, so you do,' said Vince. 'Come on with us. Reg said he's got something to tell you.'

'Oh. Okay. I suppose I can spare an hour. Just give me a few minutes to freshen up.'

The pub they chose for their meal was not the nicest place in London. In fact, Anna would have said it was very dodgy. She felt uneasy as they took their seats.

'What is it for you, Anna?' asked Reg, who waited at the bar.

'Oh, just a shandy please,' she said. 'This is . . . ' she started to say to Florentyna, but could not finish the sentence. She could hardly say the pub was nice. It was far from it. 'It's nice to be out,' she said instead.

'Yes, it is. Reg wanted to talk to you.' Florentyna seemed ill-at-ease.

'Yes, Vince said. What about?'

'Perhaps you'd best let him tell you,' said Florentyna.

Reg returned with the drinks, and Anna could not help feeling uncomfortable under his searching stare.

'The thing is, Anna, we need to bring you on board so to speak,' he said, after he had taken a sip of his pint.

'On board?'

'Yes. You see, there are certain . . .

shall we say . . . customs at Carmichael's . . . that you need to abide by. Now we all know how friendly you are with Mr Dabrowski.'

'He's my employer, just as he's yours,' said Anna, not quite liking the tone of Reg's voice.

'Yes, quite. Well . . . we've got a little money-making scheme going . . . '

'The watered-down whisky,' said Anna, feeling as though the ground had been taken from under her. 'Reg . . . ' She looked around the table. 'Vince, Florentyna, you know it's illegal. Carmichael's could be shut down if it were found we were giving guests watered-down alcohol. I've no choice but to report this. You must know that.'

'Yes, yes, Florentyna said you might say that,' said Reg. 'But . . . erm . . . I suppose that depends how much the boss knows about your little secret.'

'My secret?'

'That little redhead who was at the reception desk this morning. Pretty little thing she was. She asked if you were Anna Silverton. Of course, being a loyal friend to you, I told her you weren't. But then I spoke to Florentyna here.' Florentyna was staring studiously at her glass of stout. 'And she told me that you were. So I phoned Silverton Hall, pretending I was asking for a reference for an Anna Silverton. I had a very interesting chat with Lady Geraldine about you and what you did to her son. Oh and the theft of some money.'

'I didn't do anything to him!' Anna said, tears pricking the back of her eyes. 'And I didn't steal anything.'

'That's not what Lady Geraldine says. So the way I see it, Anna, if you keep our secret, we'll keep yours. Isn't that right, Vince?'

'Yes,' said Vince, looking at his feet as if his shoes were suddenly very uncomfortable.

'Isn't that right, Florentyna?' Reg turned to his girlfriend.

'Yes, love,' she said, looking just as unhappy as Vince.

'So we're agreed,' said Reg. 'We're all

in this together.'

'I am not with you,' said Anna. 'I want no part of your scam.'

'That's all right. I didn't think you would and I don't want to split the money any more anyway. You'll just be a good girl and turn a blind eye, won't you? Won't you?'

Anna nodded, miserably. It was all too much for her. Reg had left her little time to think about what to do. She should go straight to Janek and tell it all, whether she lost her job or not. But the secret she had kept for so long was threatening to ruin the life she had built for herself. If Reg wanted revenge, he could easily tell her step-mother where she was, and then she might be arrested.

'So,' said Reg, clapping his hands together, 'let's eat.'

'I've got no stomach for any food,' said Anna, standing up. 'I'm going back.'

'Aw, now come on, love, don't be like that,' said Reg. His vice-like grip on her hand belied his friendly tone of voice. 'You sit with us and eat some pie and chips.'

'I don't want anything.'

'I want you to stay.'

'I want to leave, and you don't want me to make a fuss in front of all these people, do you?' said Anna, tight-lipped.

'Let her go, Reg,' said Vince. 'You've gone too far, so you have.'

'We agreed . . . ' said Reg menacingly, his grip on Anna's arm tightening as he spoke.

'You agreed, and we just followed along as we always do. But I'll not stand by and see you harm a woman.'

'Oh,' Reg laughed. 'Finally getting some backbone are we, Vince?'

Vince looked up at Anna. 'I'm sorry, Anna. I didn't want it to be like this. You run along home now. Let her go, Reg, or so help me . . . '

At that, Reg did what all bullies do when confronted. He let Anna go.

As she ran out of the pub, she could

hear Vince and Reg arguing. She took one look back and saw Florentyna crying into a hankie. In her anger, she thought it served Florentyna right for getting involved with such a man.

By the time she reached Carmichael's, she was feverish and overwrought. She ran into the lift, barely noticing that someone followed her.

'Anna?' It was Janek. He quickly pressed the button so that the lift door closed, hiding them from the curious bystanders. 'Anna, what is it?'

She burst into tears and he took her in his arms. She felt safe and warm, but deep down knew that she could not enjoy that feeling for too long.

'Darling, please tell me who's hurt you?'

22

Luckily for Anna, Janek did not press the question. As if understanding she was too upset to speak, he helped her to her room and used the bedside phone to ask someone to bring up a pot of tea.

'Now drink this,' he said when the tea had arrived. 'Don't the English always feel better after a cup of tea?'

'Yes,' she said through a watery smile. 'Thank you.'

'Now I want to know who's hurt you.'

'I can't say.'

'Is it . . . ' Janek's eyes darkened. 'Is it a boyfriend? Is that it?'

Anna shook her head. 'No. I don't have a boyfriend.' She had never had a boyfriend, but she felt too embarrassed to admit that to Janek. Having a boyfriend might have resulted in her letting go of her secret in an unguarded moment and she could not risk that. Besides, for several years she had only ever loved one man and he stood in front of her, offering her tea. She could never admit that either. It would no doubt embarrass him, and make their working relationship awkward.

'Is it something that's happened at work? Has anyone been unkind to you? If they have, so help me I'll . . . '

Anna shook her head vigorously. They were getting on dangerous ground. 'It's nothing, really. I suppose it's just . . . well . . . women's problems.' As soon as she said it, she wished she had not. It was far too personal a subject to be discussing with her employer. Her face flushed bright red.

'Women's problems?'

'Yes. Women's problems.'

'Okay, well I'll admit to not knowing an awful lot about them. Do you need a doctor or anything? Painkillers? A hot water bottle? Anna, let me know what I can do to help you feel better and I will do it.'

His kindness made her want to cry more than ever. How could she possibly admit to him what had happened at Silverton Hall? He was a good man who helped people. She had seen it at Carmichael's, where he was adamant that the hotel should employ refugees and others affected by the war. He paid for all the European staff to learn English to improve their prospects, then rewarded them accordingly with better jobs when their English had improved enough so that they could deal directly with guests. It made her angry that Reg, Vince and Florentyna took advantage of that kindness. But what could she do?

She could almost see his look of horror when he learned from Reg that she had tried to harm Teddy. Janek might not believe her side of the story. In fact, he probably would not, on account of her having hidden the truth for so long. Only now did it occur to her that by keeping it a secret, she had made herself look guilty. But she was also betraying Janek's trust by not telling the truth about Reg's scam.

'I would . . . I would just like to be alone for a while,' she said, hiccoughing through her tears. 'I don't mean to be rude, but . . . '

'I understand. Sometimes when one is wounded, it's better to have time alone.'

'Now I feel worse,' she said with another sob. 'Because you really were wounded in the war and here I am making such a fuss about something so trivial.'

Janek knelt down in front of her and put his hand over hers. 'If it makes you feel this awful, then it's not trivial at all.' He reached over and kissed her head tenderly. 'I'll be upstairs if you need anything.'

When he left the room, Anna went to her bed and collapsed in a fit of sobbing, eventually crying herself to sleep.

23

When she awoke the next morning, Anna decided she would go and tell Janek everything. She owed it to him to let him know about the scam going on in his hotel, and if it meant she was dismissed because of what happened with Teddy, so be it.

Unfortunately when Anna went to Janek's office, his secretary explained that he had gone out for the morning. 'He has a meeting with the bank,' Miss Johnson explained.

'I see,' said Anna. 'When will he be back? Do you know?'

'He has a lunchtime meeting with the board of directors, probably to discuss what was said at the bank. You know they're looking to open another Carmichael's in Chicago. Mr Carmichael is coming down from Scotland, especially.'

'Oh yes, I remember,' said Anna. She had been instructed to ensure Mr Carmichael's rooms at the hotel were in order. 'I suppose I shall have to see Mr Dabrowski later this afternoon. Thank you, Miss Johnson.'

'Are you all right, Anna? You seem unwell.' Miss Johnson looked quite strident and was known to be forthright, but underneath her austere expression was a good heart.

'I am a little bit under the weather.'

'You should take the day off. Only this morning Mr Dabrowski was saying that you work too hard.'

'Did he? Well thank you.'

Anna left the office, feeling worse than ever. Janek's considerate nature filled her with guilt, along with the fact that he was so busy himself. He was always so excited when they were working on opening a new hotel. She hated that she would probably ruin his day but did not know what else could be done.

It was difficult for her not to spend

all day watching the clock, waiting until the moment that she could speak to him. When one of the staff called in sick, she took the opportunity to make herself busier, insisting she would happily deal with room service until a replacement could be found amongst the other staff.

It did help to take her mind off things, as she rushed from room to room, fulfilling the guest's demands. Most of them were pleasant enough, but there were a few who were very demanding. Anna was able to calm them down and make sure they were happy before she left. She also made sure that if anyone ordered alcohol that she brought it up from the storeroom herself. This earned her some dirty looks from Reg, but as he was stuck on the reception desk there was not much he could say or do about it.

Her final call of the day turned out to be to Mary Carmichael's suite. Miss Carmichael had lunched there with some friends, and ordered coffee. In the way of people who are used to being waited upon, Mary hardly seemed to notice who came into the room with the coffee. Anna might just as well have been invisible. Not that she really cared. She did not like Mary Carmichael, though was sensible enough to admit that her dislike was fuelled by jealousy over Janek.

The women in the room were all much of a muchness. They wore the same high fashion, the same red lipstick, and all carried the same handbags. They also all spoke in bored tones, as if life really were too tiresome.

'So?' said one of Mary's friends. 'When are you going to marry the Pole?'

'Oh darling, never,' said Mary, laughing.

'So why the rush down to London?'

'To make Jimmy Argyle jealous of course. The silly thing won't ask me to marry him, what with me being *nouveau riche*, but I know he's mad about me. And I want his title!'

'Janek has more money,' said her friend.

'Yes, and he's very sweet, but he's a foreigner, darling. Besides, he hasn't got a title.'

Anna had to bite her lip so as not to speak out. Her hands were shaking so much when she went to put the coffee on the table that the cup tilted over, pouring coffee all over Mary's skirt.

'Oh you little fool!' Mary stood up, frantically rubbing the skirt with a napkin.

'I'm sorry, Miss Carmichael. It was an accident.'

'Accident! Oh yes, you would say that, wouldn't you, Anna? Would you believe, girls, that this pale little idiot has Janek in her sights? Well you won't anymore,' Mary said, viciously. 'I'll have my brother fire you.'

'It was an accident,' said Anna. 'I'll arrange the dry cleaning for you.'

'No you won't. You'll get out of my sight, now.'

Anna fled the room and as with the night before, ran straight into Janek's arms. It occurred to her that her life would be simpler if he were not there at her most embarrassing moments.

'What's happened, Anna? Tell me,' he commanded. 'Has Miss Carmichael upset you?'

She looked up at him and realised that she could not possibly tell him what Mary had said. Mainly because she did not trust her own motives for doing so. 'It was my fault,' said Anna. 'I tipped coffee over her.'

'Yes, she did, and it was deliberate,' said a waspish voice from behind them. Anna had not realised that Mary followed her out into the corridor.

'I'm very sure it was not,' said Janek. 'Of course we'll cover any dry cleaning.'

'Are you taking my word against hers, Janek?' asked Mary. 'Really, darling. You should be careful, or there will be further talk. I don't want to have to go to my brother and tell him that your judgement is impaired, especially as he is still the major shareholder in Carmichael's.'

'Are you threatening me, Mary?' asked Janek.

'No, darling.' Mary looked contrite, but Anna felt sure it was all an act. 'Of course not. I would never do such a thing. I just think you're not thinking rationally. I'm sure you would have dismissed anyone else who tipped coffee over one of your most important guests.'

'Thank you, Mary. I'll deal with this,' Janek said coldly. 'Anna, come with me.'

Anna followed him to his office, convinced that he was about to dismiss her. His face was dark and angry when he closed his office door and turned to her. 'Now,' he said, curtly. 'Tell me what happened.'

'It was an accident, honestly,' said Anna. 'The cup could not have been on the saucer properly. If you wish to take the dry cleaning bill out of my wages . . . '

'That won't be necessary.'

'I see. Well I suppose I should get my things.'

'Why?'

'If you're going to dismiss me.'

'I don't remember saying I was going to dismiss you.'

'But Miss Carmichael said . . . '

'Miss Carmichael is labouring under a major misapprehension.'

'Yes, I know, and I'm sorry there's been gossip about us. I know you've only tried to help me.'

To her surprise, Janek smiled. 'That's not the misapprehension. But never mind that for now. What am I going to do with you, Anna? You clearly need protecting from the Mary Carmichaels of this world.'

'I can take care of myself.'

'Yes, I saw that. Last night and today. You weren't really doing a very good job of it, if I remember rightly. What's going on, Anna? This is not like you. You've been through so many things in your life, yet at the moment you look more lost than when I first met you on the train in nineteen-forty.'

'I am lost,' said Anna, with tears pricking her eyes. 'Look, you're going to fire me anyway, so I may as well tell you what I was going to tell you.'

'About what happened with Mary Carmichael?'

'No, not that.' She would never tell him that. To hear him dismissed as a 'foreigner' had broken her heart. She would not break his too. She hoped that one day he might realise about Mary Carmichael, but she could not be the one to twist the knife it. 'It's about what's been going on at the hotel behind your back. And in telling you about it, I'm going to be condemning myself.'

'What's been going on?' Janek frowned.

'It's Reg Turner . . . ' Anna hesitated. She did not really want to tell on Vince and Florentyna too. She suspected that they had both been swayed by Reg's stronger personality. Yet she had no choice. 'Reg, Vince and Florentyna have been watering down the bottles of alcohol and selling off the leftovers, then pocketing the difference.'

'How long has this been going on?' asked Janek.

'I don't know. I only realised yesterday.' Anna quickly explained about Major Dalrymple.

'So why did you not come to me straight away? Why did you not tell me last night? I presume this is what you were upset about.'

'I was confused,' said Anna. A tear rolled down her cheek. 'Reg threatened me . . . '

'He did what? Where the hell is he?' Janek made for the door.

'No, not physically.' Anna put her hand on his arm to stop him. 'Not physically. He threatened me with something that he knows about me.'

'Anna, if it's about you being illegitimate, I already know that. You told me yourself.'

Anna shook her head. 'No, that's not it. It's the real reason I had to leave

Silverton Hall. I ran away.'

'I know that too.'

'But you don't know why.'

'They made you unhappy.'

'Yes, they did. But . . . the truth is my brother fell from a tree, and he said I'd told him he could climb it, so my step-mother thinks I tried to kill him. She threatened me with the police and . . . so I took some money that Mr Stephens gave me and ran away with it. I did try to pay him back, but he can't have received it, as he is still looking for me.'

'The posters in Hyde Park,' said Janek thoughtfully.

Anna nodded miserably. 'Reg said my step-mother is still talking about having me arrested for it all. He said that if I told you about the scam, he'd tell you about me. I was going to tell you today. It's just that last night I was so confused. I'd kept the secret for so long . . . '

Janek opened his mouth to speak, but was halted by a knock on the door. 'Come in,' he said abruptly.

'Sorry to bother you, Mr Dabrowski,' said Miss Johnson, 'but the board of directors have arrived.'

'I need a few more minutes,' said Janek.

'Come on old boy,' said a voice from Miss Johnson's room. Michael Carmichael came bounding into Janek's office. 'We're waiting for the good news. Oh . . . ' He looked at Anna. 'Sorry. Mary did tell me you were dealing with this.'

'I am,' said Janek.

'Good. Good man. We don't want Carmichael's to get a bad name for service now, do we?'

Janek turned to Anna. 'I'll speak to you after lunch. But . . . '

'Oh get it over with,' said Carmichael. 'I'll do it for you if you like. You're dismissed, girl. And don't think you're getting a reference either.'

'Thank you, Mike. I said I'd deal with it.' Janek's eyes flashed angrily. He turned back to Anna. 'I *will* speak to you after lunch.'

24

Because he did not want to discuss Anna's predicament in front of Mike Carmichael, Janek had no choice but to follow his friend to the meeting room. As he did so, his lips were set in a tight line. Before they went into the room, Janek put his hand on Mike's shoulder.

'What is it, Janek?' said Mike.

'Don't you ever overrule me like that again,' Janek said.

'I'm sorry . . . ' Mike frowned, as if it was no big deal.

'You should be. I don't know what you tell your sister or the rest of your family, but it is not for you to decide who stays and who goes on the Carmichael's staff. And even if I were thinking of dismissing Anna, or anyone else for that matter, it would not be done in the callous way you just did it.'

'Yeah, I know Janek.' Mike ran his

fingers through his hair. 'Sorry, but Mary was upset. And with every right to be, I think.'

'Oh her skirt was ruined. The poor thing. But what is a ruined life against a ruined skirt, of which I'm sure your spoilt sister has many all in the same style? Mary has even less say in this hotel than you do. In fact she has no say at all, and I'll thank you to remind her of that next time you speak to her.'

'I'm still a majority shareholder until the bank says otherwise,' said Mike.

Janek shook his head. 'They've already said otherwise this morning. The transfer of shares should have gone through. Has your broker not told you?'

'No. No he didn't. But I have been travelling.' Mike took a deep breath.

'It was your decision to cash in,' said Janek.

'I know that.'

'So your dismissal of Miss Palmer is not valid. You had no right to do it. You knew the transfer would be going through soon anyway and you'd already decided to have no further say in the business.'

'Right . . . okay. So I spoke out of turn. Look, Janek, don't you think you're making rather a fool of yourself over this girl?'

'It's either that or make a fool of myself over your sister, and I know who I'd rather be a fool for. You think I don't know that your sister wants a title? Well let her have one, but if she thinks this . . . foreigner . . . has fallen for her little trap, she has another thing coming.'

Janek did not tell Anna, but he had heard everything Mary said, due to the room door being open. He had seen Anna struggle to contain the cup, but he could not understand why she did not tell the truth about what Mary said. Did she not care if he was hurt? Not that he was, but he would like to think Anna wanted to protect him. It was at that moment he realised that was exactly what she was doing. Protecting him from being hurt by Mary's words.

She obviously believed that he was in love with Mary.

He wished he could go and talk to Anna, but the board meeting was due to take place and he could not get out of it.

He took a deep breath and entered the room, standing at the head of the table and composing his thoughts. He would speak to her after lunch and help her to sort things out. 'Ladies and gentleman,' he said. 'I'm pleased to announce that from today Carmichael's hotel will officially change its name to Dabrowski's.'

25

Anna looked down at the scrap of poster that she had kept since she found it two years previously. It had a Filey telephone number. She wondered if she should phone from London or go straight to Filey.

Wanting to put as much distance between herself and London as possible, she caught a train to Filey. At least if she was there when she telephoned, Mr Stephens might not refuse to see her. She wanted to put things straight with him at least, and maybe he would tell Mrs Palmer. She had enough to pay him back the ten shillings. In fact she had enough to live for a month or two if necessary. She had saved all the money she earned whilst working for the Voronins and at the hotel, because there was very little she needed.

She had not waited until Janek came back from lunch. Believing, with good cause, that she had been dismissed by Mr Carmichael, she went straight to her room and packed a few things before leaving the hotel by the back door. She did not want Reg or Florentyna to know that she had left in case it alerted them. Reg might contact her step-mother out of spite and tell her where Anna was. She had to get as far away as possible before they realised she had gone.

Anna knew she could face Mr Stephens, but not her step-mother. If she could just convince the old butler that she had not stolen his money, at least if she ever was arrested it would not form part of the charges.

She slept part of the way to Filey, only waking when the train reached the Yorkshire moors. It was a beautiful place, and brought home to her how very little of Britain she had seen since arriving in nineteen-forty. Though not a prisoner at Silverton Hall, her circumstances had not allowed for her to go very far. She had never been invited on family holidays with her father, his new wife and her half-brother, and the staff did not get enough time off to go very far.

When she worked for the Voronins, their trips out were severely limited by having to get permission from the Russian government. She did not know for certain, but she assumed that even the pretended day trip to the seaside had to be applied for in advance in order to keep up the pretence of them going. She often wondered about them. They had not written to her and she supposed that they were not allowed to. There had been something in the news about Mr. Voronin's defection, but it had said their whereabouts were secret. She hoped they were safe and well somewhere. If they had been taken back to Russia, she felt sure there would have been something in the news about it.

Now for the first time she was seeing Britain, and she loved it. She decided that even if she were not able to see Mr Stephens, she might stay in the area for a short while and explore — at least for a week or two, until she had to find another job. That would be harder, given that she had no references and did not want Janek to know where she was. He had looked furious when she told him about Teddy's accident. Was it because she had lied to him? Or was he as horrified as she always believed he would be?

The train pulled into Filey station late in the evening. Anna decided it was too late to contact Mr Stephens. He might not want to be disturbed. So she found her way to the nearest guest-house. Not far from the station, it was called Dunromin'. She had to listen to a list of orders from the landlady, Mrs Green, before being allowed to her room.

'We're short-staffed,' said Mrs Green. 'My last girl walked out this morning, so we have to make do and mend. So no smoking in your room.'

'I don't smoke.'

'No food, and your bedding won't be changed daily. It'll be changed every other day.'

'I see. Well I doubt I'll be staying that long,' said Anna.

'That's up to you,' Mrs Green sniffed.

Anna spent an uncomfortable night trying to sleep on sheets that had clearly not been aired properly. Everything in the bedroom had a greasy feel to it, and it did not smell much better.

The following morning she went down to breakfast, only to find chaos. Some of the guests were stood at the dining room door, complaining to Mrs Green. 'We paid for breakfast,' one man said, 'so we expect to get it.'

'You'll get shown the door, that's what you'll get,' said Mrs Green, 'if you continue to talk to me like that. I've already explained to you that my girl has left me. I'm having to cook all on my own. So you'll just have to wait.'

'You're the one who told us to be

down for breakfast by eight o'clock or we'd miss it,' said the man. 'The least you could do is have it ready.'

'Can I help?' Anna asked.

'Why?' said Mrs Green. 'What can you do?'

'I've worked in a hotel and I've prepared breakfasts in another post. I'd be happy to help you in the kitchen, if you like.'

'I suppose it won't hurt,' said Mrs Green.

Anna turned to the guests. 'We're very sorry for the delay. If you'd like to wait, I'll see to it that some tea and toast is brought to you whilst the main breakfast is prepared.'

Mollified by Anna's youth and charm, the guests went back to the dining room.

'You've no rights to offer them that,' said Mrs Green.

'If I don't, you're going to lose them all, and they may even leave without paying.'

That prevented Mrs Green from

complaining any further. It seemed to Anna that the lady cared more about the money she made than making sure the guests were happy.

An hour later, all the guests had been fed, but Anna still had not eaten. 'If you don't mind, I'd like to have some breakfast now,' she said to Mrs Green.

'Don't think you're getting it or your room for free just because you've helped me,' she replied.

'Of course not,' said Anna. 'I don't suppose you've eaten either. Can I get you something?'

Mrs Green nodded grudgingly and let Anna prepare her some breakfast. 'What brings you to Filey then?' she asked once they had eaten.

'I've come to look for some friends,' said Anna.

'Men friends?'

'No, nothing like that,' said Anna. 'I'm also looking for work.'

'What do you do?'

'As I said, I worked in a hotel.' Anna

avoided saying she was the house-keeper, as she feared that the terrifying Mrs Green would think she was trying to be too grand. 'Perhaps I could help you. Until you found someone better.'

'Yes, perhaps you could. Doesn't mean you're getting your room for free though.'

'I wouldn't dream of it,' said Anna. It seemed odd, as the live-in staff at Carmichael's always had free board and lodging, but she supposed things were done differently in small hotels.

'Excuse me,' Anna said, as they washed the dishes a short time later. 'Do you know of a Mr and Mrs Stephens who live in this area?'

'No. Never heard of them.'

'Oh. It's just that they were friends of mine a long time ago. We used to work at Silverton Hall together.'

'Just a minute. Are you Anna?' Mrs Green peered at her suspiciously. Anna had only signed her name as 'Miss A. Palmer'.

'Yes, that's right. Do you know me?'

'Yes, I've heard of you.' It seemed to Anna that Mrs Green was a bit vicious when she spoke next. 'I wouldn't bother finding them if I were you. I've heard all about what you did. I'm Polly's sister.'

'Elsie?'

'Mrs Green to you.'

'Of course. I'm sorry.'

'You'll not get a welcome there,' said Mrs. Green. 'Our Polly said that if she ever set eyes on you again, she'd have you arrested. Stole some money, didn't you? Harmed a child?'

'No, that's not true,' said Anna. 'In fact I wanted to see Mr Stephens to explain to him. Did he come here too?'

Mrs Green sniffed. 'Don't know.'

'I thought you and Polly were going to run a guesthouse together.'

'We had something of a falling-out. Not really any of your business. You can work here, but I'll be deducting your board and lodge out of your wages. I don't really care what you did as long as you work hard. Stay off the street

246

and they'll not find you. I expect you to be up at six in the morning to start the breakfasts.'

And just like that, Anna had a job. She felt she had very little choice but to do what Mrs Green said, even though she did not like the lady very much. Elsie Green could not have been more different from the warm-hearted Polly Palmer.

When Anna was finally allowed to go to her room, after Mrs Green had kept her busy all day, she sat on the bed feeling miserable. It seemed that Polly was not so warm-hearted anymore. At least not towards her. She must have been very angry when Anna left.

26

'It makes sense that she would be at Carmichael's,' said Teddy. 'She knows Janek Dabrowski. He's the young man who helped her to escape from Europe. I don't know why I didn't think of that before. She always used to talk about him coming back to get her.'

Teddy and Izzy stood together looking up at Carmichael's hotel. 'I wish I'd known that when I was here last time,' said Izzy. 'It would have saved a lot of time.'

'Oh don't worry. You weren't to know. Shall we go and speak to Mr Dabrowski?'

'Yes, let's do. I do hope it was her, Teddy.'

'Me too.'

Both young people felt a little bit shy going into Carmichael's. Izzy was pleased to see that Teddy did not strut in as though he owned the place, in the way George had. Teddy had grown taller since the last time they met, and even though he was still only eighteen, medical school had matured him. He was already becoming a very handsome young man. Izzy felt a pang of regret. Because she had started to like him, she had convinced herself that he could not possibly still like her.

The man in the desk was different to the one that Izzy had spoken to the last time.

'I'm afraid Mr Dabrowski is out of the country,' he explained.

'Oh, I see,' said Teddy. 'Can you tell me when he's due to return?'

'It's hard to say. He spends a lot of time away nowadays.'

'The last time I was here,' said Izzy, 'I spoke to someone called Reg. About a girl called Anna Silverton.'

'Reg no longer works here, Miss. And the only Anna we had working here was Anna Palmer.'

'That's her!' Teddy exclaimed. 'That's

my sister. I just know it. You say 'had' working here. What do you mean?'

'I'm afraid she left too.' The desk clerk lowered his voice. 'There's been something of a shake-up. Four members of staff, dismissed. Miss Palmer, Reg the desk clerk, and two of the room service staff.'

'Anna was dismissed? Why?'

'Tipped a cup of coffee over one of our most important guests, I hear. That's not all. Before Reg left, he told me that she'd tried to murder a child years ago. Might even have killed him for all I know,' the desk clerk added salaciously. 'I know the kid's mother is still looking to have her arrested.'

'How do you know that?' asked Teddy.

'She told Reg when he spoke to her. Next thing you know, Anna's off like a shot. So there must be something in it.'

'Actually there's nothing in it,' said Teddy, clenching his hands into a fist. 'The child she's supposed to have hurt is perfectly well and standing before

250

you now. She never laid a finger on me, nor did she ever do anything else to hurt me. Perhaps you can add that to your repertoire the next time you tell this ridiculous story.'

Teddy stormed out of the hotel, closely followed by Izzy.

'Teddy,' she said, catching up with him a hundred yards up the street. 'I'm so sorry. I should have followed her and spoken to her. She'd know then that you bear her no malice.'

'It's not your fault, Izzy. I'd have probably hesitated, too, in your place. Poor Anna, thinking that the whole world is against her. Do you believe that rubbish about her tipping coffee over a guest?'

'I don't know. And even if she did, it's not the worst thing anyone has ever done.'

'I can't believe Janek Dabrowski let her down the way he did. He was supposed to be her friend. Believe me, if I ever meet that man I shall give him a piece of my mind.'

'Come on, Teddy; you don't know the whole story.'

'I know that he dismissed her when she was in trouble and had nowhere else to go. She could be anywhere now.'

'She'll be fine, I'm sure of it. What do we do now?'

'First of all I'm going to speak to my mother. She really has to put an end to this vendetta against Anna. I hate to think that because of Mother my sister feels as if she has to be on the run all the time. I want her to come home, Izzy. I'll take care of her then, just as she tried to with me when I was a little boy. She's the only person I really love in this world.'

Izzy smiled sadly. 'Oh that's nice,' she said, regretfully remembering when he used to love her too. It served her right for putting him off for so long. 'I suppose I'd better be getting back to work.'

'What? Oh yes, thanks for your help by the way. I do appreciate it.'

'I promise that if I see your sister

again I'll tie her to a chair until you get there.'

Teddy laughed. 'You always could cheer me up, Izzy. Thank you.'

27

Anna wiped her brow on her sleeve and carried on frying the bacon for breakfast. For one month she had been kept hard at work at Mrs Green's. Not that Anna was afraid of hard work, but she was used to having time to herself. Now she was lucky to have five minutes before falling into her bed and drifting off to sleep before the alarm clock woke her all too early in the morning. Even at Silverton Hall, she had often had time alone to reflect, mainly because Mrs Palmer protected her. The fact that her dearest friend no longer cared for her cut her to the quick. If only she had not left things to fester for so long.

Because Anna was so good with the guests, Mrs Green had delegated most of the work to her. The guests liked Anna, and even if she was enforcing Mrs Green's staunch rules, she was able to do so in a way that did not offend them all. As a result, Dunromin' was beginning to get a good name in the area. This only meant more work for Anna.

She could not remember the last time she had been outside and seen the sunlight. Mrs Green insisted on doing all the shopping. 'You don't want to run into anyone who might upset you,' she said to Anna.

Anna doubted Mrs Green had her interests at heart. She seldom spoke two civil words to her. The only time she did speak was to criticise, despite the fact that Anna did everything better than she did. She prepared the breakfasts, ready to carry them one by one into the dining room. She would have to do all that herself too, as Mrs Green had taken to having a lie-in, knowing she could leave things to Anna. Not that Anna minded. She found she got on much better without her employer standing over her shoulder.

What she did mind was that a good bit of her money had gone. Mrs Green had somehow managed to engineer it so that at the end of each week, Anna owed her more money than her wages allowed. She knew it was probably illegal, but with nowhere else to go, she did not know how to put things right. She barely had time to go out looking for other work, and Mrs Green had made it clear that all the other landladies in the area would not employ Anna if she left Dunromin' under a cloud.

'I've found us somewhere else,' she heard a man mutter to his wife as she passed their table. 'I mean, the girl is nice enough, but the woman . . . '

'Where is it?'

'It's nearer to the beach, but not on it. A lovely place called Anna's Return. I spoke to the landlady, Mrs Stephens, and she said we could go straight after breakfast.'

Anna almost dropped her plate. Anna's Return? Mrs. Stephens? Could that possibly be Mr Stephens's wife? And if so, the fact they had called their guesthouse Anna's Return might mean something.

'Excuse me,' she whispered, as she handed the couple their plates of food. 'I couldn't help overhearing you mention a place called Anna's Return.'

'Ye-es . . . ' said the man, looking worried.

'It's all right,' said Anna sadly. 'I don't blame you for leaving. I try my best, but . . . '

'You do that, duck,' said the man's wife kindly. 'You're a good lass and a hard worker. Lord knows why you work for that harridan.'

'I don't have anywhere else to go.' Anna had not meant it to sound as pathetic as it did.

'Well, I don't think they're looking for anyone at this other guesthouse,' said the man. 'They seem pretty well staffed there. But I could ask for you.'

'Could you? Could you also tell Mr Stephens that Anna Silverton is at

Dunromin' and if he would like to see her, she'll be waiting for him?'

'We'll tell him, duck, don't you worry,' said the man's wife.

'And please don't tell Mrs Green,' Anna whispered.

'We won't. We promise.'

Anna heard footsteps on the stairs, so moved away hurriedly. She did not want Mrs Green to catch her talking.

The morning that followed was agonising. She saw the couple leave at around eleven o'clock, then counted the minutes until Mr Stephens arrived. If he did arrive.

'What are you watching the clock for, girl?' said Mrs Green. 'Not waiting for a young man, are you? I've told you I'll have none of that. Have you changed all the beds?'

'Yes, Mrs Green.'

'Then go and dust the sitting room. It's a mess.'

'I've already dusted it,' said Anna.

'Are you defying me? I've told you I'll dock your wages if you do.'

'No, Mrs Green. I'll go and dust the sitting room.'

Having difficulty finding dust anywhere, Anna idly flicked the wooden furniture with a feather duster. She had done the room thoroughly after breakfast, and as none of the guests liked sitting around in the guesthouse, because Mrs Green was apt to scold them, it had not been used since.

She was flicking away an imaginary bit of dust when she heard a commotion in the reception area.

'She's not here, I tell you.'

'Oh yes she is. You've been working her like a slave, from what I've been told. Anna! Anna!'

'Mrs Palmer . . . ' Anna whispered. She was on her way out of the room when Polly burst into it.

'Anna, it is you!' Polly held out her arms and Anna ran into them, sobbing. 'Oh my darling girl. You've come home to me at last.'

28

'Let me help you,' said Anna, as Polly fluffed the cushions.

'You'll do no such thing,' said Polly Stephens. 'You'll sit there and rest, my girl.'

They were in the sitting room at Anna's Return, which was a much more welcoming place than the one at Dunromin'. There were still no guests around, as most had gone out to lunch, but Anna could tell by looking at the comfortable room that it was used regularly. Books littered the coffee table, and there was a half-finished game of draughts on a table by the window. At the other end was a large jigsaw puzzle, which apparently the guests added to whenever they felt like it.

As soon as Polly had arrived at Dunromin', she made Anna get all her things and return to the guesthouse with her. She had a few choice words to say to her sister too, most of which involved the return of the money Mrs Green had taken off Anna for board and lodge. Her sister had reluctantly handed over most of it, claiming to have already spent the rest.

'The Harpers said you had no work here,' said Anna.

Polly sat down next to her. 'That doesn't mean you're going anywhere else. You can live with me and Horace now. We'll find you something to do and pay you proper wages. Oh, Anna, why did you run away? I would have sorted things out for you. Not for one minute would I believe you capable of hurting young Master Teddy. Never.'

'I know . . . I was afraid because my step-mother seemed so certain I would be arrested, and I thought she was very powerful.' Anna's eyes filled with tears when she remembered that fateful day all those years before. 'I never meant to hurt him, Mrs Palmer . . . I mean Mrs Stephens.'

'You mean Polly. And I've already said that I know you didn't. You don't have to convince me, darling girl.'

'I should have guessed that you were Mrs Stephens when I saw the poster. Are you sure Mr Stephens isn't angry with me?'

'He's gone to the cash and carry but he'll be able to tell you himself when he gets back. He got the ten shillings you sent him, dear, even though he didn't want it. He never did think you stole it and neither did I. And even if you had, well you were young and afraid because of that awful step-mother of yours. As far as we're both concerned, the money was yours to have.'

'Thank you.' Anna still trembled with relief to hear that Polly had never doubted her. So much had happened over the years, and they had loads to catch up on. Mr Stephens's nephew, Richard, brought them tea and joined in, eager to hear about Anna's adventures.

'They talk about you constantly,' he told Anna. 'They've been so worried about you.'

'I know that now, and I'm sorry for it,' said Anna.

'Ah well,' said Richard. 'It's all mended now. And you'll be able to see your brother.'

'My brother?' Anna's face went pale. 'Teddy?'

'He came looking for you,' said Polly.

'Oh . . . '

'Now don't you start thinking of running away again, my girl,' said Polly.

'No, no, I shan't. I'll see him if he wants to see me. We'll bring an end to this once and for all.'

Polly nodded. 'My thoughts exactly. We're not going to let you run away from us again. Young Master Teddy is training to be a doctor now. Oh you should see him, Anna. He's grown into such a handsome young man. A nice young man too. Not stuck-up like his mother.'

Anna was able to have her first good night's sleep in ages. Having been cooped up at Dunromin' for a month, she was eager to actually see Filey.

'You go out and stretch your legs,' said Polly. 'Get some colour in your cheeks. And if you bump into my sister, don't let her bully you. You tell her it's all out in the open now, so she's nothing to blackmail you with.'

'I will,' said Anna.

She still felt a little uneasy about seeing Teddy again. Even though Polly had insisted her brother bore her no malice, she still feared that he might have been pretending to care about her just to find her. She shook her head and looked out over the sea. She would have to stop going into flights of fancy now about being locked up.

When Mr Stephens had returned the day before, he did something he had never done in all the time Anna had known him. He embraced her. What

264

was more, he apologised to her for not helping her more. But he told her he had also taken legal advice just in case they ever met her again.

'A solicitor told me that even if your step-mother went to the police now, there's no evidence against you. Young Teddy clearly suffered no ill effects from his fall. And he's not going to speak out against you, lass. So don't you worry anymore. You're safe now.'

'Thank you,' said Anna, wondering why it had never occurred to her to seek legal advice. Everything Mr Stephens said made perfect sense. 'For a clever person, you can be really stupid,' she had told her reflection in the mirror just before she went to bed. All those years wasted over something so trivial. In her own defence, at the age of eighteen, with no experience of the world, she had thought her step-mother a powerful figure who could probably make the police believe anything she told them.

Now, breathing in the bracing air at Filey, she finally felt free from the shadow that had blighted her life. She only wished she could tell Janek the truth. But what did it matter? She had been dismissed from Carmichael's; and as nothing more than an employee, she had no claim on Janek. The friendship they had known in darker times, whilst escaping from Europe, belonged to that time. It was foolish to think it could ever be recaptured or that his care for her as a child could evolve into something more grown-up when she became a woman.

No doubt Janek would continue to prosper and probably marry Mary Carmichael one day, if the young lady did not snap up a titled man instead. If not Mary, then someone very much like her: an elegant, self-possessed young woman who knew how to behave amongst high society. Anna stood at the sea front and closed her eyes, feeling the fresh air on her face. It would be easier if her feelings for Janek could be carried along on that breeze, leaving her free to get on with her life.

Sighing, she turned and made her way back to the guesthouse. Luckily she did not meet Mrs Green on the way. She supposed she would see her one day, but that was something she did not have to deal with just yet.

Strangely enough, Anna recognised the young woman first. Standing with a young man at the entrance to the guesthouse, the girl was the pretty redhead who had asked after Anna at Carmichael's. She turned and looked at Anna, her face breaking into a huge smile. She said something to the handsome young man with her. But he was not the same young man who had been at Carmichael's.

The young man turned and his eyes lit up. She saw his lips form her name. 'Anna . . . ' Suddenly the years dropped away, and she saw the child in the young man's eyes.

'Teddy!' she cried. 'Teddy, is that you?'

Brother and sister flew into each other's arms and embraced in the street, much to the amusement and bemusement of passers-by.

29

'I'm sorry if I frightened you away from Carmichael's,' said Izzy, after Anna had once again told the story of her adventures since she last saw Teddy and the Stephenses. They all sat around the lunch table in Polly's private rooms; Anna, Polly, Horace Stephens, Izzy and Teddy. Polly had prepared a ham salad, followed by sherry trifle, which they all tucked into gratefully.

'It's not your fault,' said Anna. 'It was Reg.'

'There was something smarmy about him,' said Izzy.

Anna nodded. 'I wonder what's happened to them all.'

'They were sacked,' said Teddy. 'The new desk clerk told us. And don't worry, I've made sure he can tell that Dabrowski fella that you're no child-killer.'

'Thank you, Teddy,' said Anna.

'I've spoken to Mother too. Told her she's got to stop this silliness. Father was there and he agreed with me. He'd really like to see you, Anna.'

Anna shook her head. 'I don't know . . . I know you love him dearly, Teddy, but he had plenty of chances to help me, to accept me as his daughter, but he didn't. I'm not blaming him for what happened that day, but if I'd been able to go to him things might have been different. I understand how difficult it was for him when I turned up out of the blue. At least I do now. I didn't as a child. Even so . . . I'm sorry.'

'Don't apologise, Anna, please,' said Teddy. 'You've done nothing wrong. Actually, I've got something for you that Father asked me to give you.' He reached inside his jacket pocket and took out the yellowing envelope. 'I think it might make things a bit clearer for you.'

'Clearer?'

'I don't know what's in it, but I can

guess. Go on, open it. We're amongst friends here.'

With trembling fingers, Anna opened the envelope, expecting to see a letter from her father. Except it was not that. She could hardly speak for shock. It took her a few moments to compose herself. 'Teddy, it's a marriage certificate, dated nineteen twenty-nine. Father and my mother . . . '

Teddy nodded. 'I guessed as much.'

'I always suspected it too,' said Polly. 'Only I didn't have proof. I kept trying to remind Sir Lionel, but he wasn't having any of it.'

'But that means . . . ' Anna could not finish the sentence.

'It means my mother's marriage to Father could not be legal. Unless there was a divorce, and I don't think there was. You're the proper heir to Silverton Hall, Anna. Not me.'

'Teddy! I can't do that to you.'

'It doesn't matter whether you can't or not, Anna. It's there in black and white. Or black and slightly yellow.'

Teddy smiled. 'I don't care. I'm doing well at my studies. I'll be a doctor one day. Someone useful and not some spoiled brat waiting for his father to die and leave him all his money. It's what I've always wanted.'

Anna shook her head. 'I think I can understand why Lady Geraldine was so against me now. If she knew this too . . .'

'I think she did,' said Teddy. 'She was looking for it. I think she wanted to destroy it.'

'She knew she'd married a bigamist, Teddy. If not straight away, then eventually. I'm not saying it excuses her behaviour, but it does explain it. She must have been frightened for herself and for you.'

Because the day was cool, there was a fire in the hearth. Anna walked up and went over to it.

'Anna, no!' said Teddy, standing up.

'Teddy, it's enough for me that I know. And that Father knows and has to live with his deceit. I'll not let you suffer for it as well. When you go home, tell your mother that she has nothing to fear from me.'

Anna tore the marriage certificate up and threw it in the fireplace.

'Anna, why did you do that?' asked Teddy. 'I told you it didn't matter to me.'

Anna went to him and took his hand. 'You forget, Teddy. I've been on the wrong side of the . . . blanket . . . so to speak. I know how it feels to be the outcast. I won't put you through that too. I don't care about Father's money any more than you do. But you can do great things with it when you become a doctor. Turn Silverton Hall into a hospital.'

'I promise I will,' said Teddy, putting his arms around his sister. 'But you promise me that you'll never struggle alone again. If you want anything, come to me and you can have anything you want.'

'I promise.'

'You may not think you have a family,

Anna, but you do. Me, Polly, Horace and Izzy.'

'Me too?' said Izzy, raising her eyebrows. 'Not that I'm complaining.'

'Isobel McDonald, I decided at the age of sixteen I was going to marry you. Nothing that's happened since has changed my mind. Of course, if you have qualms about marrying the son of a bigamist . . . '

'No qualms at all, Doctor Silverton.' Izzy smiled. 'I thought you'd never ask . . . '

30

The week that followed was like a holiday for Anna. The sadness she had hidden for many years began to disappear.

Teddy and Izzy stayed a few days, so the three went out and explored Yorkshire. Sometimes Anna worried that she was something of a gooseberry, when the young couple wanted to be alone, but they would not hear of going anywhere without her. She learned all about Teddy's studies in Wales, and about the hospital in London where Izzy worked.

'I feel as if I have a brother and sister now,' she told them as they walked through the Yorkshire Moors.

'You can be maid of honour at the wedding,' Izzy told her.

'Wonderful!'

'And godmother to our children,'

said Teddy. This made Izzy blush a little.

'You have to finish your studies first,' Izzy said. 'Before we get married, I mean.'

'Yes, I suppose I must,' said Teddy. 'It will be something to look forward to.'

'That's if you still want to marry me then.'

'I will, don't worry.' Teddy took Izzy's hand, and it was one of those moments when Anna felt she should not really be there.

'Shall I go on ahead?' she said. 'Order some teas at the café?'

Before they could answer, she did just that, smiling to herself. She was glad they were happy. For her there was still the shadow of Janek, but that was beyond her control. She could not make him love her so it was best to forget him.

She could only hope that one day she would find the kind of love that Teddy and Izzy shared. She had no doubt that they would marry. Teddy had told her that Izzy was his constant friend when he was alone and unhappy and it was clear that the pretty nurse adored him. She could not wish for more for her brother after the sacrifice he had been willing to make for her.

In the weeks that followed, Anna found herself smiling more and more. Being with Polly and Horace was very much like being with the Voronins, in that they nurtured her and encouraged her. They even found a job for her in the guesthouse, though she often found herself with very little to do.

'I'm worried,' she told Polly one evening over a cup of tea.

'Why? I thought everything was sorted out with Teddy.'

'It is.' Anna smiled. 'I'm worried that you've created a job for me that doesn't exist and which you may not be able to afford to pay me for. I looked over the accounts for you today, as you asked me to, and whilst you're doing well, you can't afford to spend on anything you don't really need. I could go and find work elsewhere.'

'Where would you go?' asked Polly, frowning.

'Oh I don't know. Britain is a big place. And I'm sure you'd give me a good reference.'

'Actually,' said Polly, with a gleam in her eye, 'I'd give you a dreadful reference, because I don't want you to go.' She reached over and took Anna's hand. 'We lost you once, dear. I'm not going to lose you again.'

'You won't lose me this time,' said Anna. 'I'll come and see you. Often.'

'And what if you end up working for someone like my sister? No, I won't have you out there in the world alone. Besides, you mentioning the accounts has brought something to mind. You're good at that sort of thing, and we can't really afford to pay an accountant. So why don't you be our bookkeeper and secretary? Or an assistant manager. That's it. We want to build up the reputation of the hotel and it looks good to have an assistant manager.'

'You're doing it again,' Anna said, laughing. 'Creating a job where there isn't one.'

'Give us six months,' Polly said more seriously. 'Live here and work as the assistant manager, then if after six months you still want to go off exploring Britain, so be it. Just don't go away from me yet. You know, don't you, that my first husband died before the war?' Anna nodded. 'Well we never had children, as you also know. And of course me and Horace are too old for all that. You're like our daughter, Anna. That's why we named the hotel after you. And young Master Teddy is like a son to us. We love having you both around. In fact, he said he's thinking of coming to Yorkshire to work when he's a proper doctor, so he'll be nearby too.'

'Alright,' said Anna. 'I'll give you six months. I'm not really in a hurry to go looking for other work and I love it here. I just don't want to take advantage of your good nature.'

'I wouldn't ask if I thought you were

like that. And anyway, with that nice voice of yours, it will be much better for you to deal with our suppliers. I sound like what I am. A servant. You sound like a lady.'

'You're not a servant anymore,' Anna said, squeezing Polly's hand. 'You're a hotel owner!'

'Well, be that as it may, I still feel a bit awkward when dealing with folks. So you can do it for me.'

'I'm very lucky really,' said Anna, 'apart from my step-mother and a few weeks with Mrs Green. First bringing Janek to me on the train, then you at Silverton, then the Voronins, and then . . . ' She lowered her head, barely able to mention Carmichael's. 'Yes, I've been lucky. I think my mother has been watching over me all that time.'

'I do too,' said Polly. 'And I bless the day that young man brought you to me so I could take care of you in her place.'

31

Anna ended up creating her own work. Because she had experience of helping to run a larger hotel, she was able to put some of the ideas to use at the guesthouse, but without spoiling its seaside atmosphere. Within a couple of months, Polly and Horace were relying on her for more and more. She did not mind. She liked to be busy and it was nicer to work for people who were grateful for her hard work, unlike Mrs Green.

'I think you two should sit back and relax a bit more,' she told Polly and Horace at breakfast one morning. 'Let me and Richard take care of things.'

'I wouldn't know what to do with myself,' said Polly.

'Go out walking along the front. Or up to the moors,' said Anna. 'I bet you've worked so hard you've barely seen any of them since you got here.'

'That's true,' Horace said. 'Come on, Polly, let's go out for the day. Anna and Richard and the other staff can manage.'

'Do you know,' said Polly with a big smile, 'you're right. We will. I don't think I'd have wanted to leave the place before, but you and Richard work well enough together. Maybe we'll see wedding bells soon.'

Anna smiled tightly. She liked Richard. He had become a good friend since she moved into the guesthouse, but she was not in love with him and she did not think he loved her either.

After packing up a picnic, Polly and Horace got into his little car and drove out to the countryside. It gave Anna the chance to have a good look at the books. Although both worked hard to make sure everything was aboveboard, Anna knew that sometimes, because they were so busy, things got missed. She suspected that they were paying far more tax than they needed to. She settled down in the office with a bunch of receipts and the ledger book.

Just before lunch, Richard knocked on the door. 'Anna, there's an agent here to see you.'

'An agent?'

'Yes, said he's representing some investor.'

'Okay, send him in.' Anna sighed. She hoped it was not another salesman. There were too many of them since the war, and whilst she understood that they needed to make a living, it took up too much time to deal with them.

'Miss Silverton?' said the man when he entered the room.

'Yes, that's right. How can I help you? Oh, do sit down.'

'Thank you.' He sat down in the chair opposite Anna. 'My name is Mr Allan. I'm an agent for a large company who specialises in hospitality, and we're looking to buy up quite a few businesses on this road.'

'Anna's Return is not for sale,' she said, firmly but kindly.

'We're willing to pay a good tidy sum for it.'

'What exactly do you intend to do with all the businesses you buy?' asked Anna. She hoped that the investors were not the kind who tried to push small businesses out. She had heard some nasty tales of such behaviour from Janek.

'This whole street will be turned into one big hotel.'

'I see. Does Filey need one big hotel? The holiday camp nearby already takes ten thousand people. I wonder how many more thousand could actually fit here.'

'Ah, but this hotel is special. I'm not at liberty to say who is interested in buying at this moment, but . . . '

'I'm sorry, Mr Allan. As I said, Anna's Return is not for sale.'

'Do you have the right to make this decision?' Mr Allan asked shrewdly.

Anna faltered a bit. She did not really have the right to refuse, and if the investors were willing to pay a lot for the guesthouse, she supposed Polly and Horace could retire with a lot of money. But they were not there to make the decision.

'If you would like to call again when Mr and Mrs Stephens are at home, then do so. But they have entrusted me with the business side of things and as far as I know, they have no plans to sell. I'm sure they would have mentioned it if they had.'

'When will they return?'

'I've no idea. They've gone out for the day.'

'Very well. I'll come again tomorrow. Can we say eleven o'clock?'

Anna checked the diary. 'Yes, eleven o'clock.'

She showed Mr Allan to the door and watched him as he walked down the path. Her heart sank. She would hate to see this pretty street turned into one big hotel. So much about Britain was becoming about tourism and whilst she understood it was necessary, she hated the idea of someone turning Filey town centre into a noisy entertainment centre full of arcades and dance halls.

Janek took the call from Mr Allan just after lunch. 'I'm afraid it's a no,' said Mr Allan. 'The owners were out, but their assistant manager was most insistent they would not sell.'

'Then you need to speak to the owners,' said Janek.

'That's what I intend to do,' said Mr Allan. 'I'm going to see them tomorrow at eleven. But if the girl gets to them before I do, I don't reckon much to their chances.'

'The girl?'

'Yes, the assistant manager. Miss Silverton. She's a remarkable young woman, and quite certain they won't want to sell. She doesn't want Filey turning into Blackpool, I don't think.'

'What name was that?' said Janek, sitting up straight in his chair.

'Blackpool.'

'No, the young woman.'

'Miss Silverton.'

'What does she look like?'

'Pretty little thing. Beautiful, even. Dark hair, blue eyes. Quite a looker. Do you want me to increase the offer tomorrow?'

'No,' said Janek. 'I don't want you to do anything. I'm coming to Filey myself.'

32

'Did I say the right thing?' Anna asked, for about the tenth time since the day before. She was waiting with Polly and Horace to see Mr Allan. Despite her concerns, she had not told Polly and Horace they should not sell. In fact she had suggested to them that it might be a nice retirement fund for them.

'Of course you did the right thing,' said Polly. 'We don't want these big shots coming here, turning this lovely town into a den of iniquity.'

Anna could not help laughing. 'Polly, I don't think I've ever heard the term 'den of iniquity' outside of a novel . . . and one in which there was generally lots of iniquity at that.'

Polly giggled. 'Yes, I've read some like that too, though I'm sure you shouldn't, dear. Oh, you know what I mean though. At least the holiday camp isn't too close, so we don't get all the noise. And it has its own train station. But a huge hotel, right here, in Filey itself? Oh it would be awful.'

Richard put his head around the office door. 'Gentleman to see you, Anna.'

'Mr Allan?'

'Er . . . no, his boss I think, from the sound of it.'

'Oh . . . well you'd better bring him in then,' said Anna. She stood up, as did Polly and Horace.

As the man walked in, Anna started to say, 'If you think you can bully us into selling, then . . . ' She stopped, with her mouth open in surprise. 'Janek?' Her first thought was that he was too big for the little office. And too important. Far too important.

'Hello, Anna. Do you know how long I've been looking for you?'

'Well you've found her,' said Polly, putting herself between Anna and Janek. 'But don't you go upsetting her.'

'I wouldn't dare,' said Janek with a

smile. 'Hello, Mrs Palmer. It's nice to see you again.'

'It's Mrs Stephens now.' Despite Polly's abrupt manner, Anna could see that Janek had already begun to charm her.

'I was that scraggy boy who first brought Anna to you.'

'Yes, I remember. And left her and never came back. And turned your back on her when she was in trouble.'

Janek shook his head. 'No. That's why I'm here to explain. I would have then, only Anna ran away. It seems to be something she's good at.' There was a hint of reproach in his voice.

'And what choice did she have when you left her without a job and a home?' said Horace.

Janek took a deep breath. 'I was hoping to explain all this to Anna alone, but I can see I'm going to have to get past you two first.'

'Too right,' said Polly.

'Very well. I'll explain to you all.' But he was looking at Anna. 'Michael

290

Carmichael had no right to dismiss Anna the way he did. At the time he said it, he was no longer a shareholder in the hotel. It's called Dabrowski's now, did you know?'

Anna nodded. She had seen the news of the name change in the papers.

'Yes, it's mine now. As are all the other hotels. Anyway, where was I? Yes, he had no right to dismiss you, but as I hadn't yet told the other shareholders of the changes, I couldn't say anything. Not even Miss Johnson knew, and she was in the next room. This was why I asked you to wait until after my meeting. Only by then you'd gone.'

'I can't imagine you'd have wanted me to stay, after what I told you about Teddy and stealing from Mr Stephens,' said Anna cautiously.

'Anna! How could you even think I'd believe that rubbish? I met your step-mother. Only briefly perhaps, but I saw then what sort of woman she was. And whilst I didn't fully understand what had happened with Mr Stephens,

I knew there must be a rational explanation. I know you, and I know the sort of person you are. I have known from the moment you shared your bread with me on the train. If you want me to come with you to your family and explain that, I will. I shan't let them slander you in this way. If your step-mother insists on going to the law, then I'll get you a good barrister. If all else fails, we'll run away together.'

'Oh Teddy knows,' said Anna, trying not to think of the implications of what Janek had just said. She did not want to build her hopes up. 'He came to see me the other week. It's all right, Janek. Everything's all right now.' She wanted to cry, now that everyone she cared about knew the truth, but there was still the problem of Janek's plans for the hotel. That, and her feelings for him.

'I'm glad to hear it,' he said, smiling slightly. 'Now, Mr and Mrs Stephens, please can I see Anna alone?'

'If you're thinking of trying to get this hotel,' said Polly, 'you can forget it.'

Janek shook his head. 'I'd never been to Filey before today. I flew over it a few times during the war. We used to practise up at Flamborough Head. But I've never been here. I promise you, Mrs Stephens that I wouldn't change a thing about it. I'll find somewhere else to build my new hotel. Is that all right with you, Anna?'

'It . . . it's not my decision,' she said.

'It will be.'

'Yes, I think we should go, Horace,' said Polly, with a big grin. 'Come along, dear.'

'Are you sure we should leave them alone?' muttered Horace as they left the room.

'Oh yes, I think Anna will be quite safe now.'

'Well,' said Horace, turning back, 'you just behave yourself, young man. We're responsible for this girl. I might be an old man, but I could still take on a young whippersnapper like yourself.'

'I don't doubt it,' said Janek.

Polly and Horace went out, shutting

the door after them.

'If you're asking me to come and work for you again, I can't,' said Anna. 'I have a job here.' She did not think it necessary to tell him that it might only be for six months.

'I'm not asking you to come and work for me again.'

'Oh.'

'Come out with me, Anna. Let's go for a drive somewhere. I'd like to speak to you alone.'

'We're alone now.'

'Yes, but not completely alone. Please. We'll go to Flamborough Head. It's very pretty up there.'

With no good reason to refuse, Anna got her coat and went with him. Janek had driven up in a sports car. He put the top down, and they sped through the sunshine up to Flamborough Head. It was a glorious day as they walked along the cliff tops.

'I've never seen it from this perspective,' said Janek. 'It really is beautiful up here.'

'Yes, it is. What did you want to speak to me about?'

'Can't you guess?'

Anna shook her head. She had been trying to work it out all the way there.

Janek stopped walking and turned to face her, taking her hands in his. 'Anna, I was a fool the last time we were together. I didn't like the staff gossiping about us. And for good reason. I worried about your reputation.'

'Well nothing was going on,' said Anna. 'If people want to think the worst, it's their fault.'

'The worst? Is that how you would see it if you and I were together? As the worst?'

'No, I didn't mean it like that. I meant . . . well the gossip was unkind. That's all I meant.'

'I've missed you,' said Janek. 'It's not the same at the hotel without you. My life is not the same without you.'

'I've got a job now,' said Anna. 'And I thought you said that's not what you wanted to talk about. Is it about Polly and Horace selling Anna's Return? Because they won't, and it isn't fair of you to try and put pressure on me.'

'Anna, for goodness sake, forget the hotel. Forget the guesthouse.' Janek pulled her closer to him and put his arms around her. 'I want to talk about us. I love you, Anna. I've loved you since I saw you across the road on the day I started work on Carmichael's. I saw you as a good omen. Then I went and lost you, because I was too tied up in my work. Then I found you and lost you again. I don't want that to happen anymore, Anna. I want to be with you.'

'You love me?' said Anna, her heart doing somersaults.

'Yes. If you don't love me, then say so and I'll go away and never bother you again. At least I know you're safe now.'

'I do love you,' said Anna. 'I do! That's why I went away. Mary Carmichael was cruel about you . . .'

'I know.'

'You know?'

'Yes, she didn't fool me for a minute.

But I don't want to talk about her now. Or ever, for that matter. You're far more interesting to me.' Janek put his fingers under Anna's chin and raised it towards him, kissing her with such tenderness, it brought tears to her eyes. 'Marry me, Anna,' he whispered. 'Marry me, and I promise you'll never have to run away again, darling.'

Anna threw her arms around his neck. 'Yes! Yes, I'll marry you!'

* * *

Nearly eighteen years after they had first walked up the path to Silverton Hall, as two young friends escaping war-torn Europe, Mr and Mrs Dabrowski walked towards the hall again.

Anna put her hand in Janek's, just as she had done all those years before.

'Don't worry, darling,' he said. 'You won't be staying to clean the silver this time.'

'I know. Do you think I'm doing the right thing in coming here, Janek?'

'It's up to you. If you want to turn around and leave, then we'll go. But I told you on our wedding day a year ago that if you ever ran away again, you'd better be sure to take me with you.'

Anna laughed and shook her head. 'No, no more running away for either of us. We've got even more reason to stay in one place now.' She patted her tummy.

The front door opened, and Teddy, Izzy and Sir Lionel stepped out. Lady Geraldine was nowhere to be seen, but Anna had not expected her to be there. According to Teddy, she spent a lot of time in London nowadays. Anna was kind enough to feel a little bit sorry for Geraldine, despite the way she had behaved.

Anna had woken one morning, soon after she discovered she was having a baby, and decided it was time to forgive her father. She did not want her child born into a fractured family.

Anna smiled bravely and waved at the trio at the door. Squeezing Janek's hand tighter still, in the blissful knowledge that it would always be there for her to hold, she walked towards them and into a bright new future with the man she loved.

THE END

We do hope that you have enjoyed reading this large print book.

Did you know that all of our titles are available for purchase?

We publish a wide range of high quality large print books including:
Romances, Mysteries, Classics
General Fiction
Non Fiction and Westerns

Special interest titles available in large print are:
The Little Oxford Dictionary
Music Book, Song Book
Hymn Book, Service Book

Also available from us courtesy of Oxford University Press:
Young Readers' Dictionary
(large print edition)
Young Readers' Thesaurus
(large print edition)

For further information or a free brochure, please contact us at:
Ulverscroft Large Print Books Ltd.,
The Green, Bradgate Road, Anstey,
Leicester, LE7 7FU, England.
Tel: (00 44) 0116 236 4325
Fax: (00 44) 0116 234 0205

MISTRESS ANGEL

Lindsay Townsend

London, 1357. Once a child bride, married off to halt a blood feud between rich and ambitious families, Isabella is now a tormented young widow. When her beloved son Matthew is torn away from her care, spirited somewhere into the country by her malicious in-laws, Isabella is desperate. To save her son she will do anything, risk anything. Even if it means she must lose the love of her life, the handsome armorer Stephen Fletcher . . .

THE LOOK OF LOVE

Marilyn Fountain

What happens when your impetuous step-sister goes on holiday to Italy engaged to one man, and then comes home with another? And not only that, but neither fiancé is aware of the other's existence! Before she knows it, Beth Tilney has promised to keep Lauren's double love life a secret — for now. And that's far from easy, especially when the Italian fiancé's cousin and best man, the intriguing and attractive Roberto Di Ferraio, arrives to keep an eye on things, and proves to be a big distraction . . .

MRS. CATT'S CURIOSITIES

Monica Brent

She sells anything and everything —
but more than that, she sells hope . . .
Ken Weaver has just about hit rock
bottom when he comes across Mrs.
Cart's Curiosities. And before he knows
it, he is leaving the store with a very
special purchase . . . But can an old
medal really heal a family that has
been torn apart? Meanwhile, Jay Ran-
dall has spent the better part of a
year nursing a broken heart. But thanks
to Mrs. Catt and a faded old photograph, he meets a beautiful girl named
Cece, and learns to love again.

JUNGLE FEVER

Carol MacLean

Eager to climb out from under the shadow of her famous mother, Eva manages to secure a place on a scientific expedition to the Amazon, determined to prove her own worth. But her steamy surroundings quickly build up heat of a different nature, as she finds herself increasingly attracted to the eminently desirable Dan. Then two surprise additions to the expedition turn everything upside-down. Will jealousies, family strife, and the deadly dangers of the tropics get in the way of Eva and Dan's future happiness?

RETURN TO LOVE

Patricia Robins

Sally Marsden is a girl who once had everything she wanted: a promising career as a model and Mike, a photographer, for a boyfriend — until the car accident which subjects her to months of hospital treatment for facial injuries. With her career cut short, a skiing holiday in the Austrian Alps provides a change of perspective. From here on, a young ski instructor, Johann, starts to play a major role in Sally's recovery; but by an unfortunate coincidence, Mike arrives at the same resort . . .

SICILIAN ESCAPE

Angela Britnell

Marianne Westlake arrives in Sicily desperate for a holiday after the end of her brief, unhappy marriage. She's taking refuge with her brother's old friend, Gabe Alessandro, but the long-haired teenager she remembered is now a charming international businessman and their instant attraction threatens her fragile heart. Marianne's ex-husband, Gabe's would-be fiancée, and trouble in the Alessandro family hotel business challenge them to find the courage to move on from the past and make a bright future together.